I0673205

Cover created by Deranged Doctor Designs.

A Danielle M Haas Publishing Book

Crossroads of Innocence - Injured Pride Heroes

To Mary Ann and Dick. Thank you for always supporting me and celebrating all my milestones. You're the best example of what love is, and I'm honored to be a part of your family. Much love to you both.

1

A familiar streak of long, blond hair caught Wade McKenzie's attention from across the dimly lit bar. He swallowed a groan and forced his wide smile to stay in place. Summer Clark was the last person he wanted to tangle with when the Chill N' Grill was packed and he was the only person manning the bar.

But he couldn't let his emotions show. Not when he needed to keep his costumers happy and the annoyingly persistent woman from badmouthing him all over town. Something she was known to do, and neither his reputation nor his bar could afford the bad publicity.

Not to mention she was one of his mother's caretakers. He wanted their relationship to stay in one lane, and one lane only. Something she was hellbent on changing.

Luckily, he was used to hiding behind a façade. It was easier for people to see the happy-go-lucky flirt who always had a quick comeback and smooth lines than the man who carried more burdens than he should ever have to handle.

"Can I get a whiskey on the rocks?" Chet Black, his long-time pal, settled on an empty stool and dipped his chin in greeting.

"Sure thing." Wade pivoted to the clear shelves lining the back wall and grabbed a bottle of Chet's favorite liquor. He gave a generous pour over a few cubes of ice in a short glass then slid the drink to Chet's waiting palm.

Chet took a long sip. "Place is packed."

A waitress rushed over with a drink order from a nearby table. Wade grabbed three bottles of beer and poured another whiskey before refilling an empty glass from the tap for a woman waiting at the bar. "We're slammed and I'm short-handed tonight. Not a great combination."

A delicate clearing of a throat turned his gaze to Summer's wide, blue eyes. "Sounds like you're in a pickle. Anything I can do to help?"

Wade refused to let his gaze dip to Summer's plunging neckline. He kept his focus on the customers waiting on their orders. "Appreciate the offer, darlin', but I'll rope Chet into lending a hand if I need one."

Chet snorted and tried to hide his amused smile behind his glass of whiskey. "I'm here to relax. Not work."

Wade tightened his jaw then flashed Summer a wide grin. "What can I get ya?"

She shrugged out of her jacket then lifted a slim shoulder. "How about a seat? There's not an empty one in the house."

Chet shifted on his stool.

Wade cut his gaze to the giant of a man and prayed to God he understood the meaning behind his stare. If Chet offered his seat to Summer, he'd pay one way or the other.

Chet took another sip then hunched over the bar.

A tiny thread of relief wove through the bunched muscles in Wade's neck. "Not much I can do about that. How 'bout a drink?"

Sighing, she jutted out her bottom lip and glanced around

the bar before her eyes lit. "Looks like Izzy's here. I'll take a beer and join her. Beau's a gentleman. He'll offer me a chair."

Chet made a face while Wade poured Summer's favorite ale then waited on his next costumer.

"Thanks, man," Chet grumbled over the increasing noise. "Made me look like a dick."

Wade laughed and wiped the wisp of dirty blond hair from his forehead with the back of his wrist. "Better you than me."

A broad-shouldered man with close-cropped dark hair and deep frown lines took Summer's place beside Chet. "Hopefully you can be of a little more assistance to me."

Amused by the stranger's statement, Wade leaned against the bar and cocked his head to the side. "What can I do ya for?"

Chet lifted his brows and scowled, clearly not as amused as Wade.

The man swiped his phone to life and brought up a photo. "I'm a detective from Michigan. Searching for this woman."

"You're a long way from home, Detective," Wade said.

Grim-faced, the man nodded. "Call me Toby."

Chet leaned to the side and glanced at the screen. Something in the way his eyes widened for a briefest of moments made the muscles in Wade's stomach clench. "Doesn't look familiar."

Toby turned the phone toward Wade. The bright screen showcased a blond-haired beauty with big brown eyes and the face of an angel—an angel who'd brought him more pain than he'd ever imagined possible.

His throat tightened and beads of sweat dotted his hairline. He didn't move, didn't blink, didn't breathe as he stared at the smiling face.

Jude.

Not one day had passed when he hadn't thought of her, dreamt of her. Not one day since she walked out of his life at eighteen years old and never looked back. Never called. Never returned home to her family and friends.

Never returned home to him.

Pain that'd never really left came back with a vengeance until he swore his heart would burst. He studied the picture. Her hair was longer than the last time he saw her, her face a bit fuller. But there was no denying it was Jude who stared back at him with those full lips and slightly turned up nose.

"Well?" Toby asked. "You know her?"

Intuition weighed down the pit of his stomach. He didn't know this man standing in his bar with a photo of his ex. Jude might have dragged his heart through the dirt on her way out of town, but he wouldn't betray her. At least until he knew more.

"Sorry. Can't say that I do." Swiping a dishtowel from the rack below the bar, he wiped a water spot. He hadn't lied. Jude had left town the first chance she'd gotten close to twelve years ago. The girl he'd known and loved was long gone. He didn't know the woman in the photo—not anymore.

A tiny vein ticked Toby's right temple. He shoved his phone back in the front pocket of his coat and retrieved a business card. He threw it on the bar. "I'll be in town for a few days. Call me if she shows up."

"Sure thing." Wade plucked the card between his thumb and forefingers and dipped his chin then watched the man march toward the front door.

"You all right, man?"

With his smile firmly in place, Wade shot his friend a wink and prayed he couldn't see the truth. That all it took was one mention of Jude for his entire world to fall apart.

Again.

〜

JUDE METCALF HUDDLED DEEPER into her black leather jacket and watched the cop who'd followed her back to Tennessee disappear into the cold, wintery night. She might be in front of the roaring fire in the giant stone hearth, but nothing could chase the chill from her bones.

Not after what she'd seen.

Not after she'd been chased out of her cozy apartment and forced to run for her life.

And now, after escaping the hell of her childhood, she was back in Pine Valley. Back to find the one person she could trust to help her fix the mess she'd landed in. But first, she needed to find the courage to approach him after she'd wronged him so many years ago.

Glancing over her shoulder, she watched Wade move behind the gleaming bar and memories assaulted her. How many nights had she spent in this restaurant with him, planning their futures and discovering things about herself she'd never dreamed possible? She'd gotten her first kiss in a dark corner while shooting pool, and she'd given herself to Wade fully in the room above the bar his dad had used as an office.

Her heart fluttered and heat slammed against her cheeks. Was that normal? To have such an intense reaction to mere memories of something so far in the rearview mirror? Years and hundreds of miles had separated her from her high school love, but sitting back in the Chill N' Grill, surrounded by Pine Valley's finest, made it feel like only yesterday she'd jumped on her motorcycle and done the hardest thing she'd ever done.

She'd left.

The busty blond sauntered back to the bar and a jealousy she had no right feeling swarmed inside her like angry bees. Wade flashed the woman a smile, his dimples sexier than she remembered, and filled her glass before returning his attention to Chet.

A pang of longing hummed inside her. Wade wasn't the

only one she'd left behind. She'd grown up with Chet and was glad to see he and Wade were still friends, but she couldn't get caught up in nostalgia or envy or any other silly emotion right now. Not when the stakes were way too high. She needed to put on her big girl panties and talk to Wade. He'd know what to do —could help her out of this mess so she could get the hell out of this town before anyone else found out she was here.

Drawing in a deep breath, she cast one more glance around the room. The place was full of faces from her past, so many memories that made her the person she was today, but she couldn't get pulled down by nostalgia. She'd come here with a singular goal. Dipping her chin, she hooked her bag on her back and pulled her hood over her head, she folded her arms across her chest and slid between clusters of people. Each bump or accidental elbow jab sent spikes of fear through her. She made herself as small as possible and weaved between the crowd until she reached the end of the bar.

Her heart pounded. Anxiety pitching higher than the wooden beams across the ceiling. The feeling of being watched made her skin crawl. Needing to expel some nervous energy, she tapped the toe of her sneaker against the worn floor.

Wade glanced her way and lifted a finger. "Be there in a second, darlin'."

Her knees threatened to give out. His voice was gravelly and thick as ever, and even the low light couldn't hide the captivating charm he'd had since they were kids. The small lines on his tanned face managed to make him even more handsome. Or maybe it was just the pressing need inside her to be near him.

Closing her eyes, she let her face fall forward. What the hell was she thinking? Wade might be the only person she could trust, but she couldn't do this. Couldn't stand in front of him after all this time and ask him to help her. She'd given up the right to ask him for anything the second she drove away and broke his heart.

Broke her own heart.

Because as much as she'd needed to get out of Pine Valley, it had taken every ounce of strength she had to leave Wade behind. Coming back was a mistake. She needed to keep running—keep moving until the trouble she'd found herself in stopped following.

"Sorry about the wait. What can I get ya?"

Terror and excitement grabbed hold of her vocal cords, refusing to let her speak. Her mouth went dry. She licked her lips, willing for either words to pop out of her mouth or Wade to lose interest and walk away.

"Miss.?"

Shaking her head, she opened her eyes and lowered her hood. She stared down at the weathered wood. He wouldn't recognize her. Not yet. Not with her hair dyed pink and tucked under a baseball hat.

"Is everything all right?"

The concern in his voice misted her eyes. She'd missed him so damn much. Sniffing back any more useless tears, she dashed away the unwanted dampness and finally met Wade's wide, blue eyes.

His mouth dropped, and he took a step back as if her presence repelled him. "What...what the hell are you doing here?"

2

A weird energy crackled in the air around Wade. He gripped the edge of the bar, partly to anchor himself so he didn't fall over and partly to make sure everything around him was real. He hadn't seen or heard from Jude in so long. Then within a five-minute span a detective flashes her picture with no mention of why and then she pops up like a damn ghost.

"I had to come back. I didn't have a choice."

He blinked, long and slow, as if her words didn't register. "You've been gone for twelve years. No phone call. No email. No letting me know you were alive. And now you waltz into my bar as if nothing happened?"

She winced then took off her baseball hat. She lifted her chin so the light from the neon signs bounced off the deep bruise that circled her eye. "Please, Wade. I need your help before he finds me again."

A hundred questions pounded against his brain, but only one mattered. "Who gave you the black eye?"

Jude's skin grew impossibly paler. She ducked her chin and shoved the blue ball cap back on her head, tucking in the dull pink strands of hair. She darted her gaze around, as if whoever hit her would pop up and clock her again.

"Jude?"

She winced at the sound of her name and squeezed the straps of the pack hooked on her shoulders.

His pulse picked up. Shit. He might not know why she was here, or why some random detective had flashed her photo five minutes before, but she was terrified. He couldn't let her stand around and quiver, waiting for the whatever she feared to show up. "Head upstairs. I'll get someone to cover the bar. Then we can talk."

Indecision crinkled her brow, and she bit into her bottom lip. "Are you sure?"

He glanced over his shoulder at Chet, who stared at him with recognition clear in his wide eyes. "Yeah. It won't be long before more people realize who you are. Not what you want if you're trying to stay under the radar. I'll ask Chet to cover for me and meet you in a few minutes."

She reached out as if to cover his hand with hers, letting it hover for a beat before dropping it back at her side. "Thank you."

He watched her until she disappeared behind the door to the stairwell then scrubbed a palm over his face. His whiskers scratched his skin, but the sensation barely registered. Not when his body hummed and mind raced.

Needing to snap out of the annoying stupor weighing him down, he forced his feet to carry him to Chet. Shouts for drink refills and requests from servers went unanswered. Hell, if Chet couldn't help him out, he'd close the damn bar. Something was wrong and he needed to get to the bottom of it then get Jude out of town so he could try his damnedest to forget about her all over again. He'd barely survived her leaving him the first time. He couldn't afford to get tangled up with her.

"Was that...?" Chet left the rest of his question hang in the noisy air.

Wade nodded.

Rubbing the back of his neck, Chet let out a loud whistle. "Something big must be happening. First the detective, then Jude. What's going on?"

He shrugged. "Not sure but I'm going to find out. Any way you can man the bar while I talk to her? She has one hell of a shiner. Says she needs help."

"Can you handle that?" Chet frowned, clearly not believing Wade speaking with Jude was the best idea.

"Don't have much of a choice. Can you help or not?"

"Sure." Standing, Chet downed the rest of his whiskey then hurried behind the bar.

Wade didn't have to waste time explaining the job to Chet. His buddy had helped at this family-owned bar since before he could legally buy a drink—his parents careful not to let any of the underage kids who picked up shifts after school serve alcohol. But Chet had continued lending a hand whenever needed as the years came and went, which left Wade to shoot him a quick thanks before hurrying upstairs to find Jude instead of walking him through what needed done.

The single bulb barely lit the wood-lined stairwell that led to his private room. The old stairs creaked beneath his weight, and he took them two at a time. His heart thudded harder against his chest with each step that brought him closer to Jude.

He'd imagined this moment a million times. Jude showing up at his bar. Explaining what pushed her out of town. Confessing she still loved him and asking for forgiveness.

Forgiveness his head demanded he withhold, but his heart...well that was a different story. One look at Jude had sent a tidal wave of emotions crashing over his head, leaving him shaken to the core. Shaken and furious at whoever had hurt her—had marred her beautiful skin and sent her running back to the one place she'd left behind.

Back to him.

He hesitated at the top of the stairs, nerves skittering along his spine. He could do this. Hell, he was used to putting his own needs on the backburner to help others. Wasn't that what he'd been doing his whole life? If Jude was in trouble, he'd do what he could then watch her walk away. But this time, he'd make sure to guard his heart.

Swinging open the door, Jude spun toward him with his mom's ancient Yorkipoo in her arms. "This can't be Macey."

He couldn't help but chuckle. "One in the same."

She smiled, the first since he'd laid eyes on her downstairs, and it knocked the air from his lungs.

"Well, hello, my old friend." Jude lifted the tiny mass of cream and black fur so they were face to face then placed a kiss on the dog's forehead before snuggling her close. "I remember when you were just a puppy. You were the sweetest little thing. I bet you still are."

He spared the pair another glance before shutting and locking the door then crossing the office-turned-apartment to the recliner in the corner of the room.

Jude stayed rooted in place with Macey in her arms. The bill of her hat cast a shadow over the delicate features of her face, but there was no hiding the tension rippling off her in waves. Her smile melted away, replaced by a hint of confusion. "Why isn't she with your mom?"

The question was like a punch in the gut. Macey had always been his mom's dog. He'd wanted something bigger, fiercer, but his mom insisted on the tiny dog she could take with her. Macey had fallen for his mom as hard as his mom had fallen for Macey—the two inseparable.

Until a few years ago when he'd had no choice but to turn his life upside down and do everything he could to give his mom what she needed. That included moving her from the home she'd loved for decades and into an assisted living apartment, selling his place to help with the finances, and taking in the dog who was heartbroken with the new arrangement.

But he didn't want to share everything with Jude. Not now. Not after she'd decided she didn't want to be a part of his life anymore. She'd once been the one who helped him through his problems, supported him through the challenges forced at his feet. Now she was just one more problem he had to handle.

And Lord help him, but he couldn't stop the thrill shooting through his body that she'd come back. That she'd picked him to help her.

Trying to appear more casual than he felt, he leaned back in the soft, olive colored chair and hooked his ankle over his knee. "Mama moved and couldn't take Macey with her. Now tell me what happened."

She nodded and set Macey on the floor. "Right. I'm not here to catch up. I'm here because I didn't have anywhere else to go."

Her statement sliced through his chest. So he was her last resort? He brushed aside his injured pride. "And why did you need to leave wherever the hell you've been all these years?"

She looked him in the eyes, her spine straight and chin lifted. "Because someone wants me dead."

SAYING the words out loud shook something loose, and Jude's entire body trembled. The truth had followed her like the devil on her heels since she'd left her apartment in Michigan, but she'd tried to tell herself she was overreacting. That the man who'd attacked her—the one who'd shown up at the Chill N' Grill, wasn't related to the picture she'd accidently taken.

But she couldn't hide from the bitter truth any more than she could hide from the criminal who wanted to kill her.

Wade shot to his feet, his face pinched in concern. "What do you mean? What happened?"

Fear coated the roof of her mouth, making it hard to get out the words stuck in the back of her throat. She'd only told one person what she'd seen, what she'd captured on film, and that's what started the runaway train that brough her back to Tennessee. "I accidently took a photo a few nights ago."

He frowned. "What kind of photo? And how did that lead to someone wanting to kill you?"

She held up a palm, cutting off any more questions. "Please. Just let me get this out." Rubbing her fingers along her collarbone, she sucked in a breath to calm the anxiety flapping in her gut. "I was at the pier and wanted to get a picture of the sunset. That's what I do now, by the way, I'm a photographer. The light was shimmering off the lake and it was the perfect shot. Then I noticed two men arguing. I was annoyed they were in my way, but I managed to get a few photos without them."

Wade nodded along with her words, reaffirming her in his own way that he trusted what she had to say. Something she needed more than he realized.

"When I left, a man approached me. He was in plain clothes, but he flashed a badge, assuring me he was a detective, and said he wanted to see my camera. I was caught off guard and showed him the shots I took. He tried to grab my camera, but something seemed off. No officer would act like that. So I took off. Jumped on my motorcycle and rushed home. I parked my bike in the lot and rushed to my apartment. That's when I was attacked. The detective followed me and jumped me in the hall of my apartment building."

Her fingers floated up to touch the hidden skin where the man's hands had choked her.

"Do you need a minute?" Wade ask, his voice hollow.

She shook her head and cleared her throat. "He tried to strangle me. I got away, but not before he punched me. I was in shock—in denial really. I rode awhile before heading to the police station to report everything. That's when I saw him. Standing by the front door with a group of officers. Laughing. He looked up and saw me then gave chase. Said he knew I killed that man by the lake. That I had something to do with his death. I didn't even know what the hell he was talking about. I just ran, and I haven't stopped running since."

Wade worked his jaw back and forth, agitation twitching the muscles at his temple. "Can I see the photos?"

She unzipped her bag and pulled out her most prized possession, fiddling with some buttons until the pictures littered the small screen.

Wade crossed the room and stood beside her, the heat of his body enough to turn down her nerves a few notches. She had to stop herself from leaning her head on his shoulder as he studied the scene she'd captured on camera.

"And you're sure one of the men in this picture was killed?"

She let her head fall forward, her camera left to dangle at her side. "The next day the guy's face was splashed across the news. He's dead, and I have a picture of the last known person to see him alive. I have the evidence, and clearly someone is willing to go through a hell of a lot to get it back."

"Okay," Wade said. "But one bad cop can't turn an entire police force against you. Can't keep the honest officers from coming to your aid."

A sob caught in her throat. She'd gone through the same thoughts a hundred times. "How am I supposed to know who's good and who's bad? Who'll help and who'll finish what they started? Besides, once news about that man's death hit, there was no way I could trust anyone—could convince anyone to believe me."

His frown deepened into a scowl. "Why not?"

"Didn't you talk to the detective?" she asked, throwing up

her hands, the strap of her camera slapping the air. "Didn't you ask why he was here, looking for me?"

"I was a little overwhelmed when he showed up flashing your picture. He didn't give me any details, and I didn't ask. I was trying too hard to keep my shit together. So just tell me what I need to know."

She swallowed the bile creeping up her throat. "He pinned the guy's death on me. Back in Mill Harbor, I'm wanted for murder."

3

Disbelief dropped Wade's jaw, and he lowered into a chair at the two-person table in the kitchen. He propped his elbow on the hard wood and used the tips of his fingers to keep his head upright. If his mind raced before, his brain threatened to spin right out of his ears now. "This is definitely not how I saw this conversation going."

Jude shoved her camera in her bag then swung the pack onto her back. "I get it. Showing up after so long isn't fair. I shouldn't have come here. Shouldn't have asked you to help. I'm putting you in a bad position. I'll figure something else out."

She made three strides toward the door before he was back on his feet, closing the distance between them. He grabbed her hand, spinning her around to face him. Electricity shot up his arm, kickstarting his heart and making his palms sweat. "Sorry. This is a lot to digest," he said, dropping her hand. Touching her was a horrible idea. No way he could keep his wits about him if his body hummed with anticipation and longing.

"I understand. I threw a lot at you."

He snorted. "Ya think?"

She offered a half-smile as Macey trotted to her side and nestled against her legs. "I can leave. I don't deserve your hospitality or your help."

He wanted to agree, but he couldn't force the words from his cotton-coated mouth. She'd broken his heart and turned his entire world upside down, but that didn't mean he couldn't lend a hand. Couldn't show kindness and empathy, even if it killed him to stand in the same room as her and not demand to know why she'd left in the first place.

Refusing to get tangled in the past, he focused on the current problem. He had no experience in law enforcement or criminal investigations, but he was friends with plenty of people who did. "You need to call the police."

"No. I already told you. That's not an option." Defiant as ever, she crossed her arms over her chest.

"How do you expect to get out of this mess?" He shoved his hand through his hair. "You think that detective will give up on finding you? If he chased you down here—came to your hometown to ask your old friends and family about you—he won't stop until he gets what he wants. He's proven you can't run. Can't hide. And I can't keep you safe by locking you away in my apartment forever."

Tears filled her eyes and her bottom lip trembled.

Well, hell.

Unable to resist, he pulled her in close for a hug. The familiar scent of lavender and vanilla slammed against him, bringing with it a hundred different memories of the girl he used to love. He gritted his teeth, determined to comfort her and nothing more. "I know you're scared. I want to help. But I can't do that on my own."

She relaxed against him. "I don't know who I can trust."

Keeping one arm looped around the curve of her spine, he pulled back to see her face. "You trust me, right?"

Nibbling her bottom lip, she nodded.

Her admission was a double punch to the gut. If she trusted him so damn much, why hadn't she confided in him years ago, let him help with whatever had driven her away? "Then you need to let me call my friends. This situation is bad, and it could get worse if we can't find a way to set the record straight."

"Friends?" she asked, her full lips turning down. "You said you wanted me to call the police."

"I've got a lot of friends 'round here. Things have changed since you've been gone. I don't run from the cops after throwing toilet paper in every tree in the Crawleys' front yard. I consider most of the officers on the Pine Valley Police Department close friends now, not to mention some new folks in town with more experience with this kind of stuff then you'd think possible."

Her entire body tightened, and she took a step away. "No matter how good of buddies you are with these cops, they'll notify the authorities in Mill Harbor I'm here. I can't risk it."

He shrugged. "I don't know what the proper protocol is, but I know Cruz and Lincoln will do what's right."

Uncertainty danced in her eyes. Time might have passed, but he still could read her like a damn book. She wanted to bolt, and if she did, there was no telling what would happen.

Needing a new plan, he struggled to come up with an alternative. "What if we spoke with someone you trust first?"

"You're the only one I trust." She sighed, exasperation clear on every rigid line of her body.

"What about Chet?"

The V between her light brows deepened. "What about him?"

"He was a cop. He's downstairs now. He could pop up here and you can lay out everything. Get his take. Maybe he'll have another idea. If nothing else, he'll understand how things work."

Shifting her weight, she twirled a finger along the end of her ponytail. "Chet was a police officer? Man, I'd be terrified if someone as intimidating as Chet pulled me over. Why'd he stop?"

The truth of what had forced Chet to quit a job he'd once loved twisted Wade's gut, and he turned away and crossed the room to the sink before Jude could decipher any reaction. "He quit after his wife and daughter were killed. Do you want some water?" He asked, not wanting to dive into the hell their friend had lived through.

Wincing, she dropped her gaze to the floor. "Sure."

Something changed in her voice and she met him in the kitchen, waiting for him to fill a glass from the faucet before sitting at the table. "Thanks."

He settled in the chair across from her and took a long sip of cold water. "What do you think? Can I ask Chet to come up?"

She cradled her hands around the clear glass and blew out a long breath. "Sure. I trust Chet. And I've missed him. It'll be good to see him, no matter how messed up the reason."

Her words made the muscles in his stomach clench. She'd told him she trusted *him*, ran back to *him* when she had nowhere left to turn, but she'd never said she missed *him*. He beat back the ridiculous jealousy and plucked out his phone from the front pocket of his jeans then glanced at the time. "He's working the bar. I'll shoot Chet a text and ask him to come up when things die down." Closing time was just around the corner. He'd tell Chet to let the servers know they could cash out and he'd see to everything else once everyone left.

"Okay," she said, then took a sip of water.

He sent the message then drummed his fingers against the top of the table, unsure of what to do while they waited. Jude had already confided what led her to his doorstep, and the one thing he wanted to discuss sat like lead at the back of his throat.

Coughing, he stood. Space. That's what he needed. He couldn't just sit across from Jude and pretend like everything was normal. "Hungry? I could make you something."

She scrunched her nose. "Not really."

A soft knock drew his attention to the front of the room. "Is that Chet already?"

He shrugged and hurried to the door. Maybe things had slowed down since he'd been upstairs. He swung open the door and came face-to-face with the big blue eyes and blond hair he'd been tiptoeing around for months. He skirted out to the hallway and blocked Summer's view inside. The last thing Jude needed was for the biggest gossip in town to find her in his apartment.

JUDE CAUGHT a brief glimpse of the gorgeous blond woman from the bar before Wade disappeared into the hall and closed the door. The urge to dash across the room and plaster her ear to the thin wood had her scooping Macey off the floor instead and settling the dog on her lap. "He can talk to anyone he wants. He's not my boyfriend anymore and hasn't been for a very long time."

Macey stared up with her big brown eyes as if she understood all the turmoil boiling in Jude's gut.

Sighing, Jude scratched behind the pup's furry ears. Nervous energy swirled inside her, and she tapped her toe against the floor. Time ticked by with excruciating slowness.

Wade swept back inside and offered her a tight smile. "Sorry about that."

Feigning indifference, she shrugged. "No problem."

Wade squinted, letting his gaze stay on her face a little too long, then made a beeline for the fridge. "If you're not hungry, how 'bout a beer?"

"Sure." She shoved her water to the side then took the offered brown bottle. She wasn't much of a drinker, but she'd take anything that might calm her anxiety. Doubts crept into her mind as she took a long sip. Maybe coming here was a mistake. Wade couldn't help her, and she had no right to ask him to.

So why had his name run like a mantra of salvation through her mind her entire way to Pine Valley?

Okay, so that was a thought she didn't want to examine too thoroughly.

"Does your family know you're here?" Wade asked, settling back in the chair.

Her throat tightened around the bitter ale she'd swallowed, making it burn all the way down. Or maybe it was mention of the family she'd given up everything to escape that made her blood heat. Not wanting to venture into that territory, she shook her head.

A cloud darkened his face, as if he didn't approve of not reaching out to her family. A familiar resentment tightened her grip on the cool bottle. She was used to everyone in town looking at her cookie-cutter family with admiration and respect. Two words that should never be associated with the man who raised her.

Her father was heartless and made her life hell in more ways than anyone would ever understand. Never believe. Jenson Metcalf's mission in life was to make people see only who he wanted them to see. A manipulative skill that not only created a carefully cultivated image but raised his position in the community to such heights, no one would dare speak poorly of the man who'd been elected as the mayor a record number of times.

If only others could see the devil behind the ever-present smile and disarming charm.

Another knock interrupted her spiraling thoughts. "Sounds like your girlfriend's back." The words came out tight, forced, and on a high note that didn't ring familiar to her own ears.

Tilting his head to the side, Wade gave her a hard look that made her squirm before he jumped up to answer the door.

Dammit. She squeezed her eyes shut for a beat. What was wrong with her? She'd run back to the man she'd wronged and now was throwing snide comments at him after he'd agreed to help her out of an impossible situation. She needed to get a grip and focus on fixing her problem. Then she could leave town, and this time, nothing would ever bring her back.

"Jude?"

The gruff voice turned her around and there was no fighting against the simultaneous smile and tears that took over her face. Raising, she darted across the room and threw her arms around Chet's middle. "Chet! It's so good to see you."

He stiffened for a second before engulfing her in a hug. "You, too. It's been way too long."

Something loosened inside her. When she'd fled Pine Valley, she'd been so focused on what she was escaping that she'd overlooked everything she'd miss about her hometown. Years had come and gone, and she'd never found the same type of friendships she'd left behind.

Wade cleared his throat, and he couldn't hide his irritation behind the scowl before he dipped his chin and headed to the kitchen. "Let's sit for this. Chet, I'll grab you a beer. You're gonna need one."

She dropped her arms, wishing she could have thrown them around Wade the same way she had Chet. But bridging the gap between them would be her biggest mistake of all. She needed to keep her walls high, or she'd never be able to leave town again.

Because no matter how much her heart raced at the sight of Wade, she still couldn't make her home in Pine Valley. Couldn't face the man who'd made her life a living hell for far too long.

"Tell me what's going on," Chet said, leading the way to the small table.

She explained everything all over again as Wade handed him a beer then leaned against the counter with his own drink. Both men kept their expressions hard, their attention fixed squarely on her. She fought not to glance at Wade as she spoke, choosing instead to keep her eyes on Chet's bushy beard and clean side part of his finger-length brown hair. He was so different than the tall, gangly teenager she'd last seen. But the sweet and considerate boy she'd once known was clearly still a part of him.

After she'd spilled her guts—again—she took a long pull of her beer.

"Well?" Wade asked. "What do you think? I told her we should call the police here in Pine Valley, someone we trust, to try and figure all this shit out."

Chet frowned. "Agreed."

Her chest tightened. She wanted to argue, to suggest an alternative they'd all agree was brilliant, but nothing came to mind. "Fine. One police officer. Someone you both know and trust."

Wade quirked up a brow. "Really? Just like that? I expected more of a fight."

"I don't have much fight left in me," she said with a shrug. "Besides, I came home for a reason. What's the point of asking for help if I don't take what you can offer?"

Leaning back in his chair, Chet scratched his jaw. "Who do you think? Cruz?"

Wade nodded.

"Cruz?" she asked, the name unfamiliar.

"Cruz Sawyer," Wade said. "A good, solid cop. He moved here from Nashville a while ago and we both have gotten to know him pretty well. You can trust him. I promise."

The earnestness in his voice curled her toes. "Okay."

"It's pretty late," Chet said, standing. "We should call him first thing in the morning."

Panic had any semblance of relief she'd experienced since stepping into Wade's apartment vanishing. "Morning? What do I do until then?"

Wade worked his jaw back and forth, red staining his cheeks. "You'll stay here. With me."

4

The sound of the shower sputtering to life in the bathroom cracked open Wade's eyes. The morning sun streamed through the living room window. He groaned and threw his forearm over his face to block out the intrusion. After years of closing the bar, he hated mornings. Especially ones where he woke up on the couch with every muscle in his body screaming at his poor decision.

Once Chet left the night before, an awkward tension simmered in the apartment. So much needed to be said between him and Jude, yet both had bumbled around as if they were strangers until he'd declared they should try to get some sleep. Knowing he wouldn't be able to relax no matter where he rested his head, he'd insisted Jude take his bed while he slept on the couch.

A decision he regretted after realizing her scent would be imprinted on his covers, continuing to torment him long after she left. Whatever. He'd buy all new bedding if he had to, but he had no clue how he'd get the image of her wet and naked in his shower to ever leave his overactive imagination.

Not like he had to be too imaginative. He'd seen her naked

body on numerous occasions, memorized every inch of her delicate skin down to the heart-shaped mole on her right butt cheek.

No. He couldn't do this. Couldn't lay here and think about the good times they'd shared. He sat, stretching his arms above his head, then scooped up his phone from the end table. A text from Cruz confirmed he'd be by in twenty minutes. That gave Wade plenty of time to throw on some clothes and get a strong cup of coffee in his system.

With his next moves laid out, he clamored to his feet and crossed over to the dresser shoved against the far wall by the bed. Cold shot up his legs. He really needed to buy a few rugs to place on the wooden floors. This space hadn't been meant for a long-term home, so he'd skimped on the furnishings. But with the cost of his mother's care reaching an all-time high, he needed to face the music. This would be his home for the unforeseeable future, so he better suck it up and get used to it.

As if the mere thought of his mom roused her dog, Macey lifted her head from her spot on the fluffy white pillow and stared at him with her huge, brown eyes.

He snorted. "Traitor. Slept with Jude all night, didn't you?"

Macey cocked her head to the side as if understanding every word. A trait he found as humorous as he did annoying.

He ran his palm between the dog's ears. "Let me get dressed then I'll take you outside."

Rummaging through his dresser, he pulled out a pair of joggers and a hoodie. The way the wind rattled the window told him it'd be a quick trip. Winters in Tennessee might be mild, but the cooler weather was hard on Macey. He quickly traded his gym shorts for warm pants then yanked his T-shirt over his head.

He'd felt ridiculous sleeping with so many clothes on, but any unnecessary exposed skin with Jude so close wasn't a good idea.

"Oh, I'm...I'm sorry."

Jude's stammering pivoted him toward the bathroom with his sweatshirt still in his hand. Jude stood barefoot in the hall, a pair of tight black yoga pants molded to toned legs and a fitted long-sleeved shirt showing off an area he shouldn't be looking at. Her long strands of pink hair were wet and tousled around the delicate lines of her face, her cheeks rosy and lips parted in a sexy O as she dropped her gaze to his chest.

His mouth went dry and the only thought in his head centered around throwing her ass in the bed they'd shared on more than one occasion.

"I didn't mean to intrude," she said, finally dropping her gaze to the floor. "Where should I put the wet towel?"

He shoved into his sweatshirt and snatched the damp towel from her outstretched hand. "I'll take it. I was just about to take Macey out."

"How about I start the coffee while you do that?"

"Perfect. You'll find what you need in the cabinet above the pot." He spared her a quick glance, lips pressed together, then scooped Macey off the bed. He slipped on his sneakers and hurried out the door.

Coward.

That's what he was. One sight of Jude this morning was enough to have him running for the damn hills. Or at least running for a chance to escape her presence for the first time since she'd blindsided him at the bar the night before. He just needed a little space to get his head on straight.

At the base of the steps, he jogged through the dark bar. A quick survey of the room told him he needed to give his staff a freaking raise. Last night had been hell, the place packed and understaffed. But the kitchen had run smoothly, and the servers had stepped up, even scrubbing the place clean when he hadn't been around to supervise. Choosing to stay in Pine Valley to run the Chill N' Grill may have cost him a lot—may have cost him the love of his life—but this place was in his blood.

Staying would always be the right decision.

Once outside, he sat Macey on the grassy patch of land beside the log-cabin styled bar and grill. She pranced on the frost-tipped grass, searching for the best place to do her business.

The sound of an engine motoring to life caught his attention, and he turned toward the parking lot. A black SUV with tinted windows slid out of a spot and slipped onto the mountain road, turning toward town.

Apprehension tickled his spine. He stared after the glowing taillights until they disappeared, and a Pine Valley police cruiser came into view.

Macey trotted over to Wade and whined. He lifted her off the ground and tucked her close to stop her tiny limbs from trembling.

Cruz parked his car in the spot closest to the front door and stepped out of the vehicle. His ever-present cowboy hat was perched on his head, his blue eyes full of questions. Pocketing his keys, he touched the brim of his hat. "Someone have a late night and come back for their car?"

Wade frowned. Wouldn't be the first time a patron had needed a ride home after more than a few drinks then returned the next morning. But a heaviness in the pit of his stomach told him that wasn't what happened. "Not sure, but I don't think so."

"Who do you think it was then?"

"A detective from Michigan who I lied to about a murder suspect."

Cruz's eyebrows hiked high and disappeared under the brim of his hat. "Looks like we've got a lot to talk about."

HEAT FROM JUDE'S mug seeped into her palm. Thank God she'd finished half a cup of coffee before Officer Cruz Sawyer showed up because now the French Roast burned her esophagus like acid. The cop nodded along to every word she said, not interrupting once as she finished the whole story of what had brought her back to Pine Valley.

"Okay," Officer Sawyer said, drawing out the word in a long breath. He sat back on the recliner and wrinkled his nose. "I wish you'd have given me a heads up about what I was walking into first thing in the morning."

Wincing, she set her mug on the coffee table in front of the sofa. The movement woke Macey, who perked up from her spot on the opposite end of the couch. She padded over to Jude and curled against her hip.

"Sorry, man. Wasn't sure what all to say." Wade stood beside the fireplace, his second cup of coffee cradled in his hands. "I wanted you to have an open mind when you spoke to Jude."

"Can I see the photos?" Officer Sawyer asked.

"Sure." She jumped to her feet and found her camera in the backpack. She offered the stranger who held her fate in his hands a tight smile then showed him the pictures she'd already described.

"And you're sure the detective who showed up at the bar last night is the same one you spoke with? The one who attacked you?"

She nodded. "No doubt in my mind, Officer."

He smiled. "You can call me Cruz."

She worked the name over in her mouth, unwilling to say it out loud until she knew for certain what he planned to do with the information she'd laid at his feet.

"What do you think of the photos?" Wade prodded. "Is that enough to prove she's the one in trouble?"

"It's hard to say without knowing exactly what the police supposedly have on you. What made you run?"

"When I went back to the station to report the vandalism to my apartment, I saw the detective again. As soon as he saw me, he gave chase. I was panicked and scared. He'd already hurt me once." Memories of the assault lifted her fingertips to the tender bruise around her eye. "I made it to my bike and as I drove off, he screamed that he knew what I did. That I couldn't hide."

"Interesting he'd yell this but not have more officers chase after you."

She shrugged. "Agreed, but this guy is clearly bad news. I mean, what kind of a cop hits and strangles a woman?"

Wade pushed off the wall he'd been leaning on and paced. "One who needs his ass kicked."

"Or one who's not a cop at all," Cruz muttered.

Validation tightened her stomach muscles. Something had rung disingenuous about the man who'd approached her, claiming to be a detective who was interested in her photos. But when she'd seen him at the station, laughing with other officers, she'd kicked herself for thinking she could just walk in and be believed when he was surrounded by his brothers in blue.

But here was an officer she'd never met, who had no reason to lie or trick her, who gave voice to the very thought that made her run in the first place. "Do you really think he lied?"

Leaning forward on the chair, Cruz clasped his hands together and stared at her with kind, blue eyes. "First off, Wade's right. This guy, no matter who he is, deserves to get his ass kicked. Someone who follows you home and attacks you needs to be held accountable. No questions."

Tears of appreciation stung her eyes.

"I understand your reluctance to go back to the station where this man was," Cruz continued. "Let me ask some questions. See what's going on."

"You'd do that?"

He nodded. "Do you know his name?"

"I do." Wade plucked a business card from his wallet and offered it to Cruz. "He left this with me and Chet at the bar. Told us he was a detective and looking for Jude."

"And you think this was the same guy sitting in the parking lot in his SUV when you took Macey outside?"

"Yeah. I'll pull up the security footage and see how long he was out here. It's not a coincidence he came here. Detective or not, he knew how to find you, and figured out exactly where you'd come once in town."

"What about other friends? Family?" Cruz asked. "Is there anyone else in town this guy would talk to? Anyone who would know where to find you, or accidently give him information that could be used against you?"

Her throat went dry, and she slid her palm around her mug and took another sip. Wade mentioned he was friends with this policeman, but he didn't mention how much the officer knew about who she was or her connection to the town. "I grew up here. Almost anyone would have something to tell him about me."

"And family?" Cruz pressed.

She forced herself not to flick her attention to Wade. "My brother lives one town over in Elm Ridge but would be easy to find. We're in contact from time to time. My parents and sister still live in town, but they wouldn't have much to say. I haven't spoken to any of them in twelve years."

Cruz raised his brows, unspoken questions clear on his face. "So they don't know you're here? Couldn't lead anyone to you?"

She shook her head.

A beat of tense silence filled the air. Cruz finally studied the cardstock in his hand. "Can I take this?"

"Yeah, go ahead," Wade said.

Cruz stood. "I'll start by making some calls about him. Find out if he's really on the police force in Mill Harbor. Can you bring up that security footage before I take off? I'd like to see if I can get a look at the guy's license plate. If he's impersonating an officer, the name on this card might not be real. I'll need another way to identify him."

Wade crossed over to a laptop on top of his dresser and flipped open the lid. He pressed a few buttons and carried the computer to the coffee table, angling it so they could all see the screen. "I'll start the tape from the time I went outside and rewind to see how long he was out there."

A black and white image played on the screen. The SUV parked in the corner of the lot.

Cruz picked up his pen. "Pause and zoom in so I can write down the license plate."

Wade pressed a key, waiting for Cruz to jot down the information, then resumed the video. He sped up the feed, nothing but the time stamp and occasional swinging branch moving in the frame. Then the driver's door opened and the man hustled from the SUV and moved at an unnatural speed to an old shed behind the bar then back to the SUV.

"What's he doing?" Wade asked. "All that's in that old thing is a bunch of junk."

Alarm rattled her insides. "I stashed my motorcycle in there. He knows I'm here."

5

———

Cool air whipped through the dilapidated shed and brushed against the side of Wade's face. Not like it fazed him. Hell, he welcomed the rush of cold wind. Staring at Jude's wrecked motorcycle boiled his blood. He had no doubt the man who'd messed up her bike would do the same—and worse—to Jude if he got his hands on her.

Something he would never let happen.

"I'll dust for prints," Cruz said, circling the destruction. "It's clear who did this. We have the guy on camera coming into the shed and leaving, but I doubt we have his real name. I'll make sure the area is safe before we let Jude come down and verify her motorcycle was not in this condition when she stowed it inside."

"No way this guy is a real detective. I mean, what kind of an idiot would destroy private property while working a case? This type of destruction doesn't make sense," Wade said. "Even if he was unaware cameras were set up in the parking lot, he took a hell of chance. And now, any story he's concocted to gain information about Jude is blown."

"The fact he didn't show you or Chet a badge last night

when he was at the bar was a dead giveaway for me. If I'm on an official investigation, I want everyone I speak with to know who I am and why I'm there. Anyone can manufacturer a business card, put whatever name they want on it."

Wade studied the mostly abandoned structure to make sure nothing else was tampered with or ruined. "Glad I didn't say anything when he asked if I knew her."

"Chances are high the guy already knew the answer."

Something tightened in Wade's gut. If the phony detective knew exactly where to find Jude, what else did he know?

Straightening the cowboy hat on his head, Cruz faced Wade. "So now I need you to tell me everything about this woman so I can keep her safe."

"What do you mean? She told you everything she told me." He shuffled to the opposite end of the square shelter. Cruz had become a close pal in the years he'd lived in Pine Valley, but he didn't know much about Wade except what Wade chose to show. He didn't like to expose old wounds—or fresh ones—to more people than necessary.

And where Jude was concerned, way too many people in this town were already aware of how the love of his life disappeared one night without a trace. Leaving him with a hundred questions and a broken heart—not to mention being the catalyst that fueled his inability to trust a woman.

Cruz set his feet hip width apart and crossed his arms over his chest. "You know what I mean."

Gone was the casual air of a friend, replaced by an officer who demanded answers. Resigning himself to the inevitable, Wade perched on a rusted stool shoved under a splintered counter. He grazed his fingertip over the worn material and smiled. His dad had loved this shed, building wooden birdhouses he'd give out to customers.

He shook his head to stop his meandering thoughts and

focus on what Cruz needed to know. "Jude and I have a complicated history."

"How so?"

He pinched the bridge of his nose, fighting against the mounting pressure in his head. "I've known her forever. She was my first girlfriend. I think we made it official in fifth grade," he said with a sad chuckle, thinking back on all the time he'd spent with Jude. "But we were inseparable way before that. We lived next door to her family, so she was my first friend."

Jude was his first everything, but no way Cruz needed all the details of their past.

"And what about her family? Sounds like there's a bit of a rift there if she hasn't spoken with them in so long. If I were in hot water, family's the first call I'd make."

"Not everyone has your family." A twinge of sadness pulsed along with his heart, a familiar cadence that never really left. He'd had a close family once. But then his dad had passed away, thrusting him into a life he wasn't ready for. Not long after, his mom was diagnosed with dementia, giving him a life he never wanted. At one point, his family had been his rock too, but tragedy had hit twice and smashed that rock to pieces. Leaving him alone in a world with more responsibilities than he could ever escape.

A hint of a smile lifted the side of Cruz's mouth. "True, and I thank God for them daily. But I want to know about Jude's family. Specifically, why she didn't tell them she was back in town with trouble nipping at her heels."

He shrugged, wishing he had the answers Cruz sought. Maybe then he'd understand why she'd left in the first place. "I'm not really sure. She's the middle kid. Was always close to her brother and sister. Her sister, Laura, is younger. Twenty. She was young when Jude left and never talks about it. Very close-lipped. Matthew, the brother, is more outgoing but he's not in town. I've seen him a few times over the years, but he usually avoids me."

"And the parents?"

Wade let out a long breath, the air spiraling into a haze from his mouth. Cruz wouldn't like this tidbit of information, but it couldn't be helped. "Jude's dad is Jenson Metcalf."

Cruz's jaw dropped. "The mayor?"

He nodded.

"Well, hell." Cruz lifted the brim of his hat and rubbed a palm over the top of his head, tousling his sandy brown hair before righting the hat.

"Exactly." The jovial mayor was a staple in Pine Valley, in church every Sunday with his wife and youngest daughter. Always parading around the town square. Most citizens adored him, but Wade was always under the impression Mr. Metcalf was more concerned with showing off his picture-perfect life than actually doing any real work to improve Pine Valley or the people who lived there. And a sneaking suspicion always told him Jude felt the same way.

"Well, if she doesn't want her parents to know she's in town, there's no reason to tell them. Yet."

Wade frowned. Jude would be irritated with him for exposing so much of her past to Cruz. If her overbearing father showed up at his doorstep, she'd be downright furious. "Why would you need to tell them at all?"

"If more trouble comes into town, if anyone is put in danger because of this man who followed Jude here, people need to be warned. If my first questions are centered around Jude's family, this guy will be thinking the same. He's chased her hundreds of miles. He won't just drive away because he didn't find her last night. He'll keep looking. My job is to figure out who he is and why what Jude captured on her camera is so damn important to him."

"And what do we do in the meantime?"

"She's not safe here," Cruz said, an ominous tone to his deep voice. "She needs to find somewhere else to stay."

The idea of anyone but him protecting her raised the hairs on the back of his neck. "She doesn't have anywhere else to go."

Cruz scratched his chin. "I'm going to go out to my cruiser and grab what I need to dust for prints. You should call Brooke."

Brooke Mather owned a local retreat up in the Smoky Mountains for injured law enforcement and veterans. Crossroads Mountain Retreat had been a haven for many people in trouble the past couple years, and he had no doubt Brooke would open her doors for Jude.

The question was if Jude would go.

JUDE PEEKED OUT THE WINDOW, watching Wade shake Cruz's hand then make his way toward the restaurant. Her heart pounded. He'd changed so much yet was still the same kind-hearted boy she'd grown up with.

The same boy she'd always loved.

The sound of footsteps pounded up the stairs, and she hurried to sit on the couch. The last thing she needed was for Wade to catch her pining for him.

Macey ran to the door, jumping on Wade's legs when he entered the room.

Jude hooked her elbow on the back of the couch and turned toward him. The scowl taking over his face tightened the muscles in her neck. "What's wrong?"

He slipped out of his shoes then slumped onto the couch beside her. "Your motorcycle is wrecked."

The news was like a physical blow. She had so little in this world—even less after leaving her apartment and everything she owned behind. Now, all she had was the backpack jammed with a few articles of clothing, her camera, and the bike Wade had helped her fix up right after she turned sixteen. "How bad is it?"

"He smashed it up pretty bad," he said, wincing.

She let her head fall back against the sofa. "I don't have the money to buy something else. Hell, I can't even afford to buy the parts to fix it—if that's even possible."

"We'll figure it out, but we have a bigger issue to address first."

Closing her eyes, she braced herself for what was to come. Last night had been torture. Tiptoeing around the giant elephant in the room had been exhausting and awkward. Both of them bumbling about the apartment until she'd finally escaped into Wade's bed...where a different type of torture had waited. She'd laid awake forever, replaying memories until the early morning.

Memories that warmed her from the inside out. Memories that crushed her soul and caused tears to prick the corners of her eyes.

As much as she didn't want to rehash the past, to rip open a wound that refused to heal, maybe it was for the best. To get everything out in the open so maybe they could move forward —or at least be more comfortable around each other while she was in town.

With a renewed sense of conviction, she faced him and swallowed hard. "You're right. We do have something else we need to discuss first. And for what it's worth, I'm sorry I've put it off for so long."

His eyes flew wide for a moment, mouth partially opened, before rubbing the back of his neck. His discomfort as clear as the glass candy dish on the coffee table. "I mean, yeah, sure if you want to talk about what made you leave, I'm game."

Confusion dipped her brows. "You said we had another issue to discuss first. Isn't that what you meant?"

"I meant the fact that it's not safe for you to stay here anymore."

Embarrassment singed her cheeks. She cleared her throat and smoothed a palm over her still-damp hair. "Oh. Of course. That makes sense. I'm sure I can figure something out. Especially now that Officer Sawyer agreed to look into things. Hopefully this will all be over soon. I'm sure I'll be fine. I'll just grab my things and leave. Even if I have to walk."

Needing to stop rambling, she jumped to her feet.

A soft yank on her hand stopped her progress and sent waves of heat and excitement shooting up her arm.

"Jude. Wait. You can't just leave. Not this time."

She sucked in a sharp breath, the hurt in his tone like a fist to the gut. She wanted to pull away, to run out the door and never look back. But she'd done that once and although it may have solved one problem, it had brought a whole host of others. "But you said I can't stay here."

"That doesn't mean I don't want to keep helping you." His hand still wrapped around her forearm, his touch threatened to melt her insides.

She forced herself to meet his eyes. "What do you have in mind?"

As if realizing he was still holding on to her, he dropped his hand and shoved it in his pocket. "There's a place right up the mountain—Crossroads Mountain Retreat."

"Up the mountain? Near the old camp?"

He smiled, his dimples flashing. "Actually, it is the old children's camp. The guy who owned it gave the land to his granddaughter when he died. She moved to town and turned the place into a rehabilitation center for injured law enforcement and veterans. She renovated the cabins and built a fancy new lodge. The place is full of people—staff and guests—who'll know how to protect you."

A sense of panic squeezed her chest. She shook her head,

backing away from Wade. "No. I can't go someplace I've never been with a bunch of people I don't know. It was hard enough to trust the officer you're friends with."

"I don't know what else to do. I'd suggest your parents, but..."

Her jaw tightened, anger and resentment pushed out the panic. "No. I won't go back to that house. Not now. Not ever."

He lifted his palms. "I was going to say it wasn't a good idea to go there in case you brought danger to their house, but I guess that's not an issue."

She pressed her lips together, working out what she should say before opening her mouth again. "You're right about bringing danger to people's homes. I don't want that for anyone. Hell, I hadn't even thought about how I was putting you in danger. I just showed up. And I really do appreciate everything you've done, but I can't go to some retreat and hope for the best. It's too risky."

Sighing, Wade sank down on the couch and Macey leapt into his lap. "What other choice do you have? We're running out of options, and you're a sitting duck at my place. Hopefully Cruz makes some calls and gets this whole mess taken care of soon, but until then, we have to play it safe. Have to take you somewhere—without being followed—and make sure you can't be found by this asshole."

His words rang true, but she couldn't ignore the sinking feeling in her belly. She might not know what this retreat was like, but she remembered that campground. Hell, she'd spent most summers there. The crappy cabins and overgrown trails had been ripped from a horror movie. The only good part about being there was having her boyfriend close and willing to keep her safe.

But Wade wasn't her boyfriend anymore and being alone in a dilapidated cabin deep in the forest sounded like an invitation for disaster.

She wrapped her arms over her chest. "I survived that camp every summer for years with you, Chet, and Tucker. I can do it again. I'll go to this retreat if you're sure there's nowhere else."

"There might be one other place you could stay," Wade said, scratching his chin. "Let me make a call while you get ready to leave."

Nodding, she hurried to gather the products she'd left in the bathroom and pack her limited possessions. Her stay at Wade's apartment had always been temporary, a stop along the way to getting her life back on track, but a sudden wave of grief slammed against her. Walking away from Wade the first time had been almost impossible. She wasn't sure she could do it again.

6

The old wood creaked under Jude's weight as she ascended the porch steps to the cabin-turned duplex tucked into the woods. Icy wind blasted through the trees surrounding the house, and she pulled her jacket tighter across her middle. Staying at Chet's place sounded like a good idea when Wade suggested it, but now doubts paraded in her mind. She was involving way too many people in her mess—putting too many people in danger.

And now, not only was Chet offering shelter, but his girl-friend would be caught up in her disaster of a life as well.

She hovered at the edge of the stairs. "Are you sure Chet's okay with this?"

Wade snorted and placed a hand on the small of her back, ushering her to one of the front doors. "Have you ever known Chet to agree to anything he didn't want to do?"

A half-smile lifted her lips. "No, but I haven't seen him in twelve years."

"Not as much has changed 'round here as you'd think." He winked then knocked on the door.

Woof! Woof!

She took a step back, concerned the dog on the other side would barge through the barrier any second.

"Don't worry. That's Wrigley. He wouldn't hurt a fly unless that fly attempted to take out Mia. Who, by the way, you'll love."

A lump lodged in her throat at the name of Chet's girlfriend. She never imagined Chet would be with anyone besides Laurie, and as much as she tried to keep away from Pine Valley and everyone she'd left behind, news of Chet's family's deaths had trickled her way. She should have come home then, should have set aside whatever hard feelings kept her away, and been there for her friend. She hadn't wanted to admit all the things that had kept her away, but now, the true reason was blaringly obvious.

Cowardice.

That's right. She could avoid her family, refuse to speak with the father who'd done so much damage, but she wouldn't be able to stay away from Wade. Clearly she was like a moth to a flame when it came to her high school love. And somehow that flame burned brighter and hotter twelve years later.

How was that even possible?

The door flung open, ripping her from her wayward thoughts. A curvy woman with tight black curls that touched the top of her shoulders and kind, brown eyes greeted them with a wide smile. A hip-high grey and black spotted dog barked at her side.

"Wrigley, stop. I'm sorry. He gets excited. Especially when Wade's here. Wade usually brings food." Mia shooed the dog behind her, sneaking outside while riffling through a packed key ring. "I'll leave him home while we check out the apartment next door."

"Next door?" Jude asked.

"Yeah, this way you're close but have your own space. Is that all right?"

Appreciation warmed her from the inside out. "Perfect. This is incredibly nice of you."

Mia pushed into the attached apartment and waited for Jude and Wade to step inside before offering her hand. "I'm Mia by the way. Nice to officially meet you."

Jude had to fight an overwhelming urge to hug the woman and took her offered palm instead. Must be the fact she'd kept everyone away for so long that was making her want to act like a mushy mess. Or maybe it was the fact that every fiber of her being wanted to touch Wade in any way she could, but her survival instincts had her keeping her distance. Which made everyone else around her fair game. Thank God she hadn't done something stupid when Cruz had offered his help.

"I'm Jude. It's nice to meet you."

Wade shuffled his feet in the doorway, indecision clear on his pinched face. "I've got some things to take care of. You okay here?"

Her stomach dipped all the way to the floor. Being near him made her feel safe. But that wasn't fair. He had a life to take care of. Dropping everything and babysitting her wasn't an option. She forced a smile. "I'm fine, thanks."

"I'll be back later. I'll bring dinner if that's okay with you."

She nodded.

As if sensing the tension, Mia elbowed him onto the porch. "Bring enough for me and Chet. He's working all day and I've got a mess of paperwork. Last thing either of us want is to cook after a busy day."

Wade cracked a smile. "Fried chicken for four."

Jude groaned. "The famous Sunday night fried chicken from the Chill N' Grill?"

"One and the same," Wade said.

Saliva instantly pooled in her mouth. "Thank goodness you're right and some things haven't changed around here."

He retreated a step then stopped. "Stay alert. Be safe."

Mia threaded her arm in Jude's. "Wrigley and I've got her."

Wade cast one more glance at the duo before turning and jogging down the stairs.

A familiar pang of longing reverberated through her heart, but she didn't get a chance to dwell on it. Mia released her arm then shut and locked the door.

Jude spun around to take in her surroundings. The living room flowed into a small kitchen. A stone fireplace took up the far wall and a sliding glass door led out to a deck. The furnishings were sparse—a threadbare sofa with a chipped coffee table in front of it and a cream-colored armchair that had seen better days—but it was clean and well kept. She swung her backpack off her shoulder and sat it at her feet. "This is really very nice of you and Chet. Do you own the duplex?"

"Nope. I used to live here, Chet next door. We drove each other crazy," she said with a small laugh then shrugged. "But fate and tragedy threw us together. Now we live at his place. We rent from Bob Truly. We told him we need the extra space for a few days, and he gave his permission. No questions asked."

The name of the local hardware store owner sent a new wave of nostalgia crashing over her. "He was always the sweetest man."

"Still is." Mia glanced around and frowned. "Do you have any more luggage?"

Embarrassment made her palms sweat, but she met Mia's concerned stare head on. "I don't know what all Chet told you, but when I left my apartment, I didn't have time to grab my things. What's in the bag is all I have, along with a motorcycle that's been wrecked."

It wasn't pity that tightened the lines of Mia's smooth skin, but a look of understanding—of a shared experience Jude was unaware of.

"I'll bring over some clothes. They might be a bit big on you, but they're clean and comfortable. I have some extra toiletries too, if you want them. Then we can figure out what else you need and the best way to get it."

Jude bit her bottom lip to stop any more tears from forming. She'd left behind more than one family when she ran away, and now at least the one made from bonds of friendship was willing and eager to welcome her back with open arms. Helping her pick up the pieces of her broken life any way they could.

Which would make it all the harder when it was time to leave again.

WADE ALLOWED himself one brief glance in his rearview mirror as he drove along the tree-lined lane and turned back down the mountain toward home. With his wrist draped over the steering wheel and elbow propped on the door, he let out a bone-rattling sigh. Twenty-four hours ago, Jude was a mere echo of memories that continued to haunt him. Now, she was here. In Pine Valley. And driving away had been more difficult than he'd anticipated.

But he couldn't wallow in any of his memories, or the mess Jude had brought into town. She was hidden and safe, and he had a business to take care of. Sundays were always busy—folks coming in after church and most people in town wanting their weekly fix of fried chicken. The kitchen wasn't where he usually spent his time, but he made it a priority to get in early on Sundays and do as much prep work for his team as possible.

None of that changed because Jude was back.

Following the curve of the mountain, his phone rang and snapped him from his thoughts. He cast a quick glance at the name on the screen on the dashboard then pressed the button on the wheel to answer the call. "Hey, Cruz. What's up?"

"You drop off Jude?"

"Yeah. I made sure to take the scenic route. No one followed. Chet lives out in the middle of nowhere, so I would have spotted a tail."

"I'd feel better if she would have agreed to stay where Brooke could keep an eye on her. Mia's tough as hell, she's proven that, but she's not trained to deal with something like this."

Wade tightened his grip on the wheel. "I agree, but Jude can't be talked into much. She's already uncomfortable being back in Pine Valley. The idea of being surrounded by a bunch of people she doesn't know or trust was too much for her."

Cruz's disgruntled sigh rattled the speaker. "Well, it is what it is. I'm glad she's tucked away, but that's not the only reason I called."

The sudden drop in his friend's baritone lifted the hairs on Wade's arm. "What happened?"

"Nothing, yet. Just confirmed what we already assumed. Toby Whitehead isn't a police officer or detective. I reached out to the Mill Harbor Police Force. I didn't mention Jude or the murder she told us about. Just asked for Detective Toby White-head. The woman I spoke with had no idea who I was talking about."

He thought back to what Jude said about the man parading around as a member of law enforcement. "Could he work for a different town? Jude mentioned she saw him talking with officers outside of the police station."

"Doubt it, but it's possible. Could also be the name he put on the business card is bogus. Doesn't want anyone down here to know his real identity."

A tension headache pulsed against his forehead. Figuring out who had attacked Jude then chased her home was key to ending this nightmare. "What about his license plate, or the prints you grabbed from Jude's bike?"

"I tossed that information at Lincoln. I wanted to touch base with you before I reached back out to him."

Irritation climbed up the back of Wade's neck. He appreciated being in the loop, but Cruz wasn't relaying any relevant information. Cop or not, the asshole had tried to kill Jude and needed to be caught. "Has anyone in town seen this guy? I mean, we know what he's driving and what he looks like. In a town this size, he'll stick out like a city boy in my bar."

"I've got all eyes on the lookout. I wouldn't be surprised if he ditches the car though. Unless the guy's an idiot. He knows you saw him pull out of the parking lot this morning, and it would only be a matter of time before we figured out he destroyed private property."

Wade groaned as he turned into the lot and parked in his usual spot.

"Lincoln's calling on the other line. I'll be in touch."

Wade ended the call and slumped forward, resting his head on the wheel. He'd been on the periphery of a lot of scary shit the last year or so. He'd witnessed people he cared for in pain, in danger, and with their lives on the line. But it'd never hit so close to home. A crippling fear threatened to steal his wits. He wasn't equipped to deal with a situation like this.

Okay. Enough of the pity party. Get your ass out of the car, get on with your day, and do your damn job. Cruz has this under control. Everything will work out.

Pep talk given, he hopped out of his truck and hustled toward the restaurant. The cold air slapped against his cheeks, but he stopped and stared at the structure that was more familiar to him than the back of his own hand. His great-grandfather had built the log cabin when he'd first moved to Pine Valley. Needing to make an income, he'd combined his passion for hunting in the mountains with his passion for cooking and created a destination for locals and travelers alike. A down-home watering hole with kind servers, good food, and cold beer.

The bar had been passed from generation to generation. Wade had grown up loving the bar and grill that would one day be his, never once resenting the hours spent toiling away after school or in the summer. This was his home away from home before it'd become his permanent place to live.

But even though this place was in his blood, nothing could have prepared him for the day his dad had unexpectedly died. Leaving his overwhelmed mother to manage a restaurant while grieving the sudden passing of her husband. For Wade, it hadn't mattered if he was only eighteen years old. His future held only one path.

Even when Jude had asked him to run away with her. To leave this town and never look back. He'd loved her with his whole heart, but he'd picked his home. His family. The second half of his heart.

Blinking away the stupid tears his sudden wistfulness had brought on, he rushed inside, desperate to escape a painful past and the memories that never faded.

A dark figure sat at the bar, his back to the door.

Wade stopped, his heart thudded against his breastbone. Before he could grab his phone, a man swiveled around and faced him. "Hello, again. Are you ready to tell me what you know about Jude Metcalf?"

7

Jude slipped out of her black boots and carried her bag to the round table set up in the small kitchen. She plopped it on the scarred wood and took a seat. The space was clean and tidy but being alone with only the hum of the appliances made gooseflesh erupt on her arms.

What was she supposed to do now?

Drumming her nails against the table, she took stock of her temporary home. Being left in a house that wasn't hers was off putting—like she was invading someone else's space. But wasn't that exactly what she'd done since driving into town last night? Invaded everyone's space, dropping her troubles on their doorstep? First Wade and now Chet and his girlfriend.

Maybe she should leave. Officer Sawyer was on the case. She didn't have to stick around while he figured things out. Staying in town would just keep a target on her back.

Her phone vibrated in her pocket. Sighing, she checked to see who was calling before answering. "Hey, Matthew."

"Hey, yourself. What the hell's going on?"

Even her big brother's irritation couldn't keep the joy from expanding her chest at hearing his voice. He was the only tie to her family she kept firmly knotted. A lifeline she leaned on as often as she could.

"What do you mean?" she asked, feigning confusion. She hadn't told him about coming back to town. There was no reason to involve him in her mess. He'd spent too much time looking after her as it was.

"Mama called me. She's freaking out. Said some detective came to the house and was asking questions about you."

Alarm straightened her spine. "What? Tell me exactly what Mama told you."

"Some guy showed up and wanted to know if she'd seen or spoken with you. Said you're in big trouble and he needs to find you right away. What happened? Are you all right? Where are you?"

Each question ripped through her chest like a bullet—sharp and explosive. She squeezed her eyes shut for a second. Shit. Shit. Shit. She'd been so concerned about her safety, and the safety of those who'd stepped in to help, but she'd never considered her family.

Her father... well he could burn in hell for all she cared. But if the past had proven anything, it was that Jenson Metcalf wouldn't go down without a fight.

Or a chance to turn the tables and make everyone else the bad guy while he bounced between his role as victim or savior.

Swallowing her panic, she opened her eyes and focused on organizing her spiraling thoughts. "I'm okay for now. Some things happened up in Michigan and I got scared and ran."

"Ran where?" Matthew asked. "Do you need me to come get you?"

Appreciation misted her eyes. "I'm in trouble. I saw something I shouldn't have and now that detective—or at least that's what he claims to be—is after me. He's dangerous."

A beat of silence pulsed over the line. "Did he hurt you?"

Tears streamed over her face. "Yes."

A light tap on the door sounded before Mia let herself in. Her grin quickly fell away. "Are you okay?" she mouthed.

Jude wiped the moisture from her face and nodded. She held up a finger, indicating she needed a minute.

"Sonofabitch. Tell me where you are," Matthew demanded, a hardness to his words she seldom heard from him. "I'm tired of all this secrecy. Of you being all alone, prancing all over the country. Let me bring you home. You can stay with me and Brandon. Mom and Dad don't have to know. But please, let me help you."

A lump lodged in her throat. A part of her wanted to accept his offer to crash with her brother and his husband. The other rebelled against the thought of relying on him or anyone else in her family. Matthew had always been her champion, but that didn't mean he'd escaped their father's clutches. Jenson still lingered on the periphery of Matthew's life, waiting for a chance to pounce and reclaim the son who'd strayed. She'd fought too hard for too long to just toss up the white flag and return to a place of uncertainty and fear. "I'm safe. That's all you need to know right now."

"Jude..." He drew out her name like he had when they were kids.

"Listen, I'm taking care of this. I don't want you or Brandon or anyone else to be caught in the middle of my mess. When the dust settles, I'll let you know. Hell, I'll even come and see you. I miss you."

"I miss you, too. And I'm here. Always, okay? I don't care about the trouble, or the mess, or whatever the hell this is. I care about *you*."

The lump in her throat tripled in size, making it hard to breathe. "I love you. I'll be in touch."

Disconnecting, she wiped her eyes and cleared her throat. "Sorry about that."

Mia took a step further into the room, her dog beside her,

and she set a giant tote bag at her feet. Clothes spilled over the sides. "No need for apologies. I'm sorry you're going through this. I might not know the details, but I do know what it's like to be thrust into a situation where control is ripped away and you're afraid of what's around each corner."

Her words piqued Jude's curiosity. "What happened to you?"

Mia scrunched her nose, as if trying to decide how much to share. "That's a very long story, and one that's not only mine to tell. Let's just say I survived the darkest, scariest time of my life and came out the other end with more than I ever expected."

"You mean Chet?"

Mia grinned. "Trust me, I never thought I'd fall so hard for a guy who was nothing but a pain in my ass for months. But things worked out for us, and I'm sure with Cruz helping out, things will work out for you too. I don't know what caused you to leave Pine Valley, but Chet's happy to have you around. Hopefully I'll get to know you a little while you're here."

Mia's genuine kindness lowered Jude's guard. She'd once had so many friends, people always around to lean on, but that had changed the minute she left town. Her job had her bouncing around the country most of the time, always in search of more inspiration. Friends weren't something she had many of. It'd be nice to reconnect with old ones, and possibly make a new one or two, while she was in town. "I'd like that."

"Good," Mia said. "But first, here are some things. Once you go through them, we can see what else you need and figure out the best way to get it."

Jude stood, and the dog wiggled his butt to her side and pushed his nose against her hand. "He's a handsome boy."

"He's handsome all right, but his bark's a hell of a lot worse than his bite and everybody knows it."

Jude laughed as Wrigley tried to lick her face. "I'm sure he could do some damage if someone threatened you."

A hint of emotion skittered across Mia's face before she schooled her expression with a jovial smile. "Hopefully I never have to find out. I've had all the threats I can handle for one lifetime."

Her words sent a shiver down Jude's spine and made her realize she wasn't the only one with a past. Hopefully Mia was right, and one day she could look back and say the darkest parts of her life were behind her. But a sinking feeling in the pit of her stomach told her she had a long way to go before that could ever happen.

WADE'S HEART shot to his throat. He staggered forward a bit, not wanting the man who'd called himself Toby to sense his trepidation, but not quite sure how to play things. His gut told him to act like he was unaware of who this guy really was and what he'd done. Admitting even the tiniest bit of knowledge would only dig the hole he was in even deeper. "Well, mornin'. I guess you didn't see the *Closed* sign on the door."

The man shrugged, not an ounce of chagrin on his weathered face. "Maybe you should lock up when you leave. Would keep people from just walking in."

Regaining his stride, he flipped on the lights and crossed to behind the bar. He didn't want to get too close to this man—he'd proven how dangerous he was—but Wade kept a hunting rifle hidden beneath the cash register. He'd never had to use it outside taking down game on the mountains, but he'd feel a lot more confident if a weapon was within arm's reach.

"Small towns like this, I don't get many people breaking into my place of business." He reached into his memory for the moment he and Jude had left earlier. Rushing out without locking up wasn't out of the realm of possibility, but not securing his home after everything that had happened was farfetched.

"Oh, I know small towns. Which is one reason I know you lied to me last night."

Wade tightened his jaw. "I didn't lie." Keeping an eye on the man, Wade busied himself wiping down the bar and gauging the diminished supplies he'd have to refill before he opened.

"You're telling me you don't know Jude Metcalf?"

"That's not what I said." He threw the white dishcloth over his shoulder, inching closer to the gun. "You showed me a picture and asked if I knew who it was. The woman in the photo didn't look familiar. So what's the problem?"

"The problem is I *know* you and Jude have a long history."

He stilled and looked the man dead in the eyes. "Then you'd know I haven't seen or talked to Jude in twelve years. That's a long time. A lot changes. So if you're telling me Jude is the woman in the picture, I can tell you she didn't look like the girl I once knew."

A pinch of sadness squeezed his chest. Jude wasn't just different in appearance. He hadn't heard her infectious laugh or seen her easy smile since she'd crashed back into his life the night before. A lot of that could be the fear that brought her here, but something deeper lingered in her eyes. Something kept her closed-up and distant. A part of him wanted to smash down the walls she'd never had before and get to the heart of the problem. The other part screamed to leave things alone. That it wouldn't be worth the pain of losing her again.

"Listen. You seem like a nice guy. I don't want any trouble. I'm just trying to do my job, and part of that job is finding Jude Metcalf and holding her accountable for her actions." He hooked his jacket to the side, exposing the handle of a black handgun. "I'd hate to think you're giving me the runaround."

With his pulse pounding, Wade pressed his fists against the bar and leaned forward. "Are you threatening me, Detective?"

The man smiled. "Nah. Just making myself clear."

The desire to lunge across the bar and strangle this asshole had him grinding his knuckles harder into the smooth wood. "Noted. Now, if you'll excuse me, my staff will be here any moment and I have a million things to do before we open."

Wade held his ground, refusing to budge as he kept his smile in place and gaze fixed casually upon the stranger in front of him.

"You still have that card I gave you?" the man asked, standing.

"Sure do."

He dipped his chin. "Good. I'll be around."

The statement came out as more of a threat. Wade stayed glued to his spot until he was alone, then rushed to lock the door. A whole lot of people would be upset, but no way he could open today. Not with adrenaline rushing through his veins and a psychopath on the prowl.

With a trembling hand, he snatched his phone from his pocket and called Cruz.

"Hey—"

"The guy was at my bar," Wade said, cutting off Cruz. "Let me rephrase that. He broke into my bar. Was here when I got back from dropping off Jude. His vehicle wasn't in the parking lot. A blue sedan was. I can try to pull up the plates on the security footage."

He glanced through the window, but the man had already disappeared. Shit. He should have kept a better eye on him. Then he could have at least told Cruz which direction he'd fled. Switching gears, he headed for the back room where a computer was set up.

"This guy is more dangerous than we imagined," Cruz said. "Lincoln got some details. His name is Benji Blitz. Has strong ties to a well-known crime family from Detroit. The Strombiskis. The family's been pushing their business into Northern Michigan."

"Shit." Wade shoved a hand through his hair then stroked a few keys to bring up the video feed.

"It gets worse," Cruz said. "The men in the photo—one of them is a part of the family. The top boss's nephew. Jude has photo evidence of the nephew with a man right before he was murdered. This couldn't just put one man behind bars. It could take down an entire crime family."

—————

8

"Dammit," Wade muttered into the phone. A fresh wave of fear slammed against him as he pulled up the security feed in the small office off the kitchen. The blue sedan appeared on screen, a clear shot of the license plate visible. "This just went from bad to worse, didn't it?"

"Yeah," Cruz said. "It did. This guy's more dangerous than we thought. He's not just a common criminal. His ties to the mafia make him an even bigger threat. Did he hurt you? Damage any of your property—either the bar or upstairs in your apartment? We already have a list of crimes to pin on him, but the more ammunition we can use the better."

Wade shot to his feet, knocking the chair backward to the floor. The clattering sound rang against the bare walls. "I didn't even think to check upstairs."

"I'm pulling in the parking lot now. Let me in then we'll head up together."

Wade disconnected the call and rushed to the glass door. He watched Cruz jump out of his cruiser and jog to the entrance of the Chill N' Grill. He let Cruz in, then locked up and ran toward the stairwell. A cold sweat broke out on the back of his neck. A man who'd hit a woman might not have any qualms about hurting a dog. If Macey were hurt, he'd never forgive himself.

Pushing into his private quarters, his heart lodged in his throat at the mess waiting to greet him. Cushions were tossed off the furniture, the quilt ripped from his bed, and cabinets cleared of all their contents. Piles of fractured dishes and shredded paper littered the floor.

He took another step inside, surveying the damage and searching for his mom's dog. "Macey?" he asked softly. "Come here girl." He listened for any clue of where the dog could be.

A tiny whimper sounded from the corner of the room, behind his bed, before Macey bolted forward.

Crouching low, he opened his arms, and she capitulated her shaking body against him. He stood and rested a steady palm on the back of her head. "It's okay, girl. I got ya. Everything's okay."

"Sonofabitch." Cruz swept his cowboy hat off his head. "I'm sorry, man. This sucks."

Wade shrugged and held Macey closer. "Nothing that can't be replaced. Could have been worse, but why do this? Why come up here and trash my place?"

"My bet is the guy's got one hell of a temper. Probably came up here hoping to find Jude, or at least something to point to where she is. When he didn't find anything, he went nuts. Destroyed your place the same way he did Jude's motorcycle. Sends a pretty clear message he's unhinged and pissed."

Wade picked his way past the debris. He righted one of the kitchen chairs and sat. "And if he's working for some well-known criminal organization, he was sent here to do a job. One he probably has no choice but to finish."

"Exactly. Families like the one we're dealing with don't take kindly to things—or people—slipping through the cracks. Especially when finishing a job means bringing in the evidence, and witness, that could put one of their own behind bars."

"He won't stop until he finds Jude," Wade said, swallowing past the terror wedged in his throat.

Cruz crossed the room to stand in front of him and rested a heavy hand on his shoulder. "We won't let that happen."

Wade dropped his head forward. "She's got so much stacked against her. How can we keep her safe?"

"First, that's my job and I'm damn good at it. Jude might have left Pine Valley for whatever reason, but it's clear she has plenty of people in town still in her corner. Willing to fight for her. And one thing I've learned from my time in this town, we're more than capable of taking care of our own."

A sad smile lifted the corner of Wade's mouth. The pep talk was needed, and a damn good one, but it didn't make the butterflies in his stomach dissipate.

"We also have some good news," Cruz continued.

Wade lifted his gaze, eyes wide. "What's that?"

"I called Mill Harbor PD again after I found out what we're dealing with. I gave them more details, while being careful to omit Jude's name. Detective Hocking assured me they don't believe Jude killed anyone, but they want to speak with her."

Apprehension tickled the back of Wade's neck. "I'm not sure if she'll go for that. She was adamant she didn't want any police involved. Getting her to speak to you was like pulling teeth."

"Maybe we can at least get her to make a copy of the picture she took. That might be enough to appease the police up in Mill Harbor but keep her from putting herself in harm's way."

"I'll ask her." Wade sighed, the impossibility of events weighing him down. All the times he'd imagined Jude coming back into his life, he'd never once thought she'd bring so much turmoil. All he'd ever wanted to do was make Jude happy, to help her in any way he could, but now that she was here, he didn't have a clue how he'd keep her safe.

"I can come with you, if you'd think it'd help."

"No thanks. I'll clean this place up a little then head to Chet's. She'll want to know what you found out, and I'll mention the picture. If she thinks it will help put an end to all this she might jump on board."

"Do you want some help?" Cruz glanced around the wrecked room.

"Nah. You have more important things on your plate, and this shouldn't take me too long. Don't have much stuff."

Firming his lips in a thin line, Cruz nodded then left with a promise to keep in touch.

Sighing, Wade carried Macey over to her plush dog bed beside the fireplace and set about righting his apartment. Anger hummed through him. He'd dealt with his fair share of tough blows, but he'd never been violated this way. Never had a stranger tear apart his world piece by piece in search of the one thing that had always meant more to him than anything.

Jude.

He found the broom and his chest tightened. Jude had certainly crashed back into his world like a wrecking ball. Too bad he couldn't pick up the broken parts of his life as easily as the cracked dishes.

A BARK of laughter cramped Jude's stomach. Snorting, she covered her mouth with her hand and gasped for air. She couldn't remember the last time she sat and enjoyed talking with someone—enjoyed a simple moment of plain fun. "You're kidding? Chet said that and you still ended up moving in with him?"

Grinning, Mia rolled her eyes. "What can I say? I can't resist a grumpy recluse with a heart of gold."

The description of her old friend sobered Jude. She tucked her feet under her on the armchair and took a sip of hot tea Mia had made. "He was always quiet. More reserved than the rest of us. I hate to think of him as grumpy and reclusive."

Mia shrugged. "I understand now that was a defense mechanism. A way to cope with everything that happened with Laurie and Riley. What he lived through would have destroyed most people."

Jude cradled her warm mug in her hands and stared into the flickering flames of the newly built fire. "I should have come home when I heard about what happened. I should have been there for him."

"He wasn't ready to let anyone be there for him for a long time," Mia said. "You're here now, and for however long that is, be his friend. I might not know you well, but I can tell you're a good one. It'd be nice to have you around for a while. Chet would love hearing us giggling through the walls."

She grinned at the image of Chet pissy and irritated while he tried to relax in the attached apartment. But that was a fool's dream. She couldn't stay, no matter how badly she wished it was a possibility.

A soft knock on the door turned her attention to the front of the room.

Wrigley jumped from his spot curled beside Mia on the couch and barked.

Jude frowned. "Is that Chet?"

"Doubt it. He's working at the retreat all day. Won't be home until after dinner is served, which won't be for another six hours or so." Mia stretched onto her feet and hurried to the front window, peeking through the blinds before her shoulders relaxed. "It's Wade. He's usually slammed on Sundays. What in the world is he doing here?"

A ridiculous lightness fluttered in Jude's core, and she rose to her feet as Mia let Wade inside. The scowl on his handsome face quickly sent the flutters packing and anxiety crept in to take its place.

"Sorry I didn't call, and I hope it's okay I brought Macey." He hefted the small dog he held in his arms. "I didn't want to leave her alone."

Wrigley bolted forward and whined, as if Macey had been brought for him to play with.

"Of course you can bring her," Mia said, scooping Macey from him and holding her close.

The little dog trembled and burrowed under her chin.

"What's wrong?" Every tight muscle in Wade's body screamed that something bad had happened.

He rubbed his palm over his face. "My apartment was ransacked. Macey was scared to death. It's not safe for either of us to be there."

"Oh my God," Jude stammered and sank back down to the chair. "Do you think it was the detective?"

"I know it was because he was waiting for me at the bar when I got back. And he's not a detective. Cruz made some calls. The police in Mill Harbor have never heard of the guy. Gave a fake name and a fake business card."

She shook her head, words escaping her.

"That's awful," Mia said.

"I have a bag in my truck," he said, hooking his thumb over his shoulder. "Figured I'd call Brooke."

"Can you stay here?" Jude asked, finally finding her voice. She hated the way her words shook, as if her need to have Wade close were broadcasted for all to see.

Mia darted a questioning look between the two of them then set Macey on the floor, where she pranced around Wrigley, tail wagging. "Chet and I have plenty of room for you at our place, or even here, but it's whatever you two are comfortable with. Why don't I head into town and grab the items Jude still needs while you two talk?"

"You don't have to do that," Jude protested. "You've already done too much."

"I haven't done anything besides spend an enjoyable morning with a new friend." Mia slid the list of things Jude still needed off the table and tucked it into the front pocket of her jeans. "You can't head into town and shop for yourself, so I'll do it for you. I'll be back soon. I'll leave Wrigley here, if that's okay. He can probably protect you more than Macey."

"Hey, she bites harder than you'd think," Wade said.

His attempt at humor made Jude smile despite her churning stomach. "Remember when she was a puppy and always chomped on your fingers? I swear she thought they were hot dogs."

The side of Wade's mouth hitched up. He held up his hand and wiggled his fingers. "I'm still offended by that."

An awkward silence fell over the room. Mia cleared her throat and ran a palm over Wrigley's head. "Well, anyway. You be a good boy, and I'll be back soon. Call if you need anything."

Wade stepped aside and let Mia leave then locked up behind her. "So, about where I'm staying tonight. Do you really want me to stay here? With you?"

She swallowed hard and ignored the deafening beat of her heart. She didn't need to expand upon her request. Didn't need to tell him that being near him made her feel safe, made her feel whole. She didn't need to confess he wiped away bits of longing and sadness she could never outrun. All she had to do was give a simple answer.

"Yes."

He dipped his chin and a flicker of the boy she used to know flashed along with his dimples. "Okay then. I'll go out and grab my bag and my rifle real quick."

"Your rifle?"

Scrunching his face, he rubbed the back of his neck. "I grabbed it from behind the bar. I can leave it in the truck if it makes you uncomfortable."

The idea of having a loaded gun so close made her nervous, but she was probably being silly. Wade wanted to protect her, which was sweet, but...

"I can tell you don't like the thought of me bringing the gun inside. I'll leave it in the truck. Be right back."

She watched him go and a shiver of excitement ripped through her. Another night spent with Wade might lead to more trouble than she was already in.

9

Jude stared out the sliding back door at the small pond that lay beyond the deck. A thin layer of ice coated the water, beams of sunlight sparkling off the surface. Naked branches of the surrounding trees swayed with the breeze.

The sound of the door closing behind her set her nerves on edge and calmed her anxiety at the same time. How the hell was that even possible? She missed the days when being alone with Wade was as natural as breathing.

Those days were long gone, and now she was looking at hours of uninterrupted time with the man she should be staying far away from. Because as much as she understood she was the one who'd walked away, he was the one who'd refused to come with her.

She winced at the familiar bite of pain from the memory of his rejection before turning away from the serene picture outside.

Wade dropped his duffel and let it land at his feet. "How you holdin' up?"

She shrugged, trying to pinpoint the cascade of emotions

flowing through her. "Scared. Confused. Overwhelmed. I'm antsy as hell and feel like I need to do something, but I can't. I can't leave, can't ride my bike to unwind, can't wrap my freaking mind around this crazy plot twist that's derailed my life."

"Who says you can't leave?"

"Where am I supposed to go?" she asked. "It's not safe to go anywhere. As nice as it is that Chet and Mia are letting me stay here, I can't help but feel a little trapped."

Hooking a thumb in the front pocket of his jeans, he shifted his weight. "We could go for a walk."

"Really?"

"Why not? I mean, no one knows you're here, and this is private property. We won't venture far. Maybe head out back and make a lap around the pond? The dogs will like it."

"Well, if the dogs will like it, who am I to say no?"

Chuckling, he dug Macey's leash and a tiny red puffer vest from his bag and put them both on the dog.

She snorted out a laugh. "Seriously?"

"Don't make her feel self-conscious," he said, shooting her a smirk. "She doesn't like the cold. If I don't put this stupid thing on, she's got five minutes in her, tops."

Wrigley ran to Macey and sniffed at her jacket as if he'd find a treat tucked inside.

"Does he need a leash?" she asked, glancing around for something she could use to tie onto his camo collar.

"Nah. Tucker trained him. He'll stay close."

Frowning, she laced up her sneakers and threaded her arms through her black leather jacket. "Tucker trains dogs?"

"Yep. He works at the retreat I told you about. Another old pal who went into law enforcement—K9 unit. He now runs the canine therapy for Brooke. Does a damn good job. He tried to help me with Macey once I had her full time, but she's pretty set in her ways."

She kept her questions to herself as she stepped onto the

deck and descended the stairs. He hadn't mentioned much about his mom, a woman she'd loved as much as her own mother, and she was dying to understand why Wade now had her dog and lived above the bar. Convenience might be a factor, but the old office space wasn't meant for permanent living. A nagging feeling told her there was more to the story than Wade had shared, but it wasn't her place to ask.

Once on the lawn in the backyard, she lifted her face toward the afternoon sun. The pressure squeezing her chest loosened. She needed this. Needed to be outside, soaking in the mountain views and feeling the rush of nature. The air might be cool, but the sunshine beamed down and heated her skin just enough to tolerate the wind.

"Beautiful," Wade said.

His thick, gritty voice had her shifting her position and dropping her gaze to meet his. "Excuse me?"

The sudden pink of his cheeks had nothing to do with the bite of the breeze. He scratched at the whiskers on his chin. "The day. It's a beautiful day. Chilly, but pretty."

The slight stammering of his words lifted her lips. She could let his statement go and pretend like she didn't understand he'd been talking about her. But she'd always loved watching him squirm. And something about being back in this town, back in these woods with him, made her act a little more impulsively—a little more like the girl she'd left behind. "You're a horrible liar. Always have been."

He grinned. "A pretty girl's standing in front of me, I've got to say something."

She tilted her head to the side and fought not to widen her smile. "All that boyish charm's gonna get you in trouble one of these days."

The amusement fled from his face and he changed direction, heading for the narrow path that wound around the pond. "Trust me. I stay as far away from trouble nowadays as I can."

She rushed her pace to fall into step beside him. "And here I am, bringing it to your doorstep. I'm sorry about that. I didn't think about the danger, and I should have."

Wrigley jogged ahead, his nose pressed to the ground.

He stopped and faced her. The ice on the pond beyond him shimmering. He tucked his bottom lip between his teeth, as if the motion would help him think. Something he'd done since he was a kid. "I'm glad you came back, even if the reason sucks. A part of me thought I'd never see you again. No matter what happens from here on out, I'm happy to have a chance to at least leave things with you on a better note."

She hated she'd hurt him, but a bite of resentment had her wrapping her arms over her middle—creating a physical shield around her battered heart. "I never wanted to say goodbye to you. Ever."

"Then why did you?"

The question stalled her breath. A million reasons—a million instances—had pushed her to run away. But it was Wade's refusal to run with her that made her never look back. Unable to stare into his sad eyes without spilling her guts, she continued walking along the water. She'd answer his question, but she wouldn't tell him everything.

She couldn't.

"I ran because I was dying here." She wished the pain she carried inside could dissipate as easily as her admission that came out on in a spiraling puff of air.

He caught her by the crook of the arm and turned her toward him. "Dying? In Pine Valley? What does that mean?"

She ran her fingers along the base of her neck, the familiar feeling of panic cutting off her windpipe. Abuse came in many different shapes and sizes. It came in ugly words and accusations, in the withholding of love and acceptance. Child abuse was something she'd lived with for so long, the fear of her father ingrained in her from her earliest memories, that she hadn't even recognized it. Hadn't realized that even though she didn't carry bruises, it didn't mean that her father's behavior hadn't left scars.

Scars she feared no one would ever believe she carried.

The slamming of a car door echoed against trees. Wrigley halted, his ears pinned back and tail rigid.

Her eyes widened and she stilled. "Who's that?"

Wade surveyed the area. "I don't know, but we should take cover."

He offered his hand.

She hesitated for only a second before she gladly accepted and followed him into the dense brush of the surrounding trees.

WADE'S PULSE pounded as he pulled Jude deeper into the forest, Macey tucked into his arms. Leaves of most of the trees were long gone, leaving bare branches and not nearly as much cover as he'd hoped. A few evergreens dotted the landscape, and he rushed for the pointy needles, the smell of sap strong and potent.

"What about Wrigley?" she whispered, staying close behind him.

He maneuvered Jude so her back was pressed against the thin branches protruding from the thick trunk. He stood in front of her, peeking to see where the hound had gone. "He's sniffing around the pond."

Jude's teeth chattered. "Could Mia be back already?"

"I doubt it. It'd be a quick trip, but not impossible. I'll call and find out." He searched for his phone then checked the screen. "Shit. No service."

The crunch of delicate footsteps reached his ears, as if someone was trying to stay under the radar, and he stilled.

Jude's eyes widened.

He lifted a finger to his lips, his mind spinning. Why had he brought her outside? He didn't have a weapon to protect her. Couldn't do a damn thing if some mob-connected criminal had found her and planned to ambush them in the woods.

But he wouldn't go down without a fight. Wouldn't stand here and wait for someone to hurt Jude. "Stay here. I'm going to see if someone's there."

She latched onto the neck of his sweatshirt. "Don't go. I'm scared."

He rested his hand over hers, the touch of her skin instantly warming him down to his toes. "I'll be back. Take Macey." He loosened her grip and passed over the trembling dog.

She nodded. "Okay. Be careful and be quick."

He flashed her a tight smile then surveyed the area beyond their hasty hiding spot. Wrigley had made his way to the side of the house, his gait slow and steady. Chances were if someone was skulking around the property, Wrigley had caught their scent and was headed in the right direction.

Without thinking, he pressed a quick kiss to Jude's cheek and darted away from the tree. He stayed as concealed as possible, his breath hitching high in his throat as adrenaline pumped through his system.

Wrigley stopped and lifted his nose in the air, one of his front paws aimed forward as if pointing to something in front of him.

More rustling sounds tightened his nerves, and he moved toward a patch of bushes that would give him a better view of the front of the house. He stayed low, fear tensing every muscle in his body.

A flash of blond hair peeked from under a blue, knit hat. Tall, brown boots stomped along the side of the house and the woman he'd been avoiding outside of her frequent phone calls about his mother used her hand to shield her eyes as she stared into the backyard.

His stomach dropped. Someone wasn't here for Jude, she was here for him.

Swallowing a groan, he stood and lifted an arm over his head. "Summer."

She turned his way and smiled wide. "Wade! There you are. What are you doing in the woods by yourself?"

Summer might not be a criminal with a weapon, but she could be just as dangerous for Jude if she spotted her. No doubt everyone in town would soon know Jude was here and where she was staying. He had to make sure Summer didn't figure out his real reason for being at Chet's.

Needing to make sure Jude wouldn't be seen by Summer, he jogged forward, positioning himself so he faced Jude's hiding spot. "Hey. Just out for a little fresh air. What are you doing here?"

Summer rushed toward him, her smile never wavering. "I was worried about you. Last night you seemed off then disappeared. Now the Chill N' Grill's closed, which never happens on a Sunday. I tried to call, but there was no answer. So I thought I'd track you down and make sure you're okay."

Her concern should flatter him, not annoy him, but he couldn't help his reaction. He'd made it clear for months he wasn't interested in deepening their friendship but she wouldn't take the hint. Either that or she thought she could change his mind. Something that would never happen.

A thought struck him, and fear squeezed his throat. If Summer had found him here, so could anyone else. "How did you know where I was?"

She shrugged. "You were with Chet last night so my first thought was you'd be with him today."

He let loose a long breath. Okay, so she hadn't followed him without being noticed. She'd used logic, even if it was a little disconcerting.

"What's wrong? Aren't you happy to see me?" She made her voice high and a little babyish, which held no appeal for him.

He forced a smile. "I'm always happy to see you, but it's been a weird couple days."

"Luckily it looks like you've got the day off and you can tell me all about it." She tugged his elbow and pulled him forward. "Let's get out of the cold, grab some lunch or something. I promise, I'm a good listener."

He walked beside her, relieved to steer her further from Jude. "Thanks for the offer, but I can't."

She pressed her lips into a pout and pivoted to the side, her line of vision now pointing straight at Jude. "Why not?"

Shit.

Looping his arm around her shoulders, he aimed her back toward the front of the house. "Because I promised Chet I'd do some things for him. Will take me a couple days, probably. And since I had to close down the restaurant for electrical reasons, I figured it was the best time to lend him a hand."

She wrapped an arm around his waist and snuggled against him. "Anything I can help with?"

He winced, hating the tightrope he walked. He gave her a quick squeeze then increased his pace to put some space between them as he rounded the corner of the cabin and made a beeline toward her car. "Afraid not. I appreciate the concern though. You're a good friend."

Reaching the driver's side door, he pulled it open for her, making sure there was no mistaking this impromptu rendezvous was over.

She sighed and climbed inside then stared up at him with big, blue eyes. "Fine. I guess I'll see you later then."

"Sure. Drive safe." He closed the door and waved as he watched her drive away.

10

A woman's sugary sweet voice had Jude chancing a peek around the sappy pine tree. Heat crashed against her cheeks. The pretty blond from the night before rushed toward Wade, her excitement clear as the early-afternoon sun in the blue sky. Wade met her, both too far for their words to carry to her on breeze.

She gritted her teeth and held Macey close. She should stop watching, should sink back against the tree and wait for them to finish speaking. But she couldn't tear away her gaze.

Wade hooked his arm over her shoulder and Jude saw red. When the blond looped her arm around his waist, the urge to tear the woman's limbs from her body nearly had her running across the lawn. Instead, she pressed her back against the tree and sank to the ground. Pine needles brushed against her skin. Sticky sap slid against her jaw.

Macey whined and trembled in her arms.

"I'm sorry, girl," Jude said, tucking the dog into her jacket to keep her warm. "We'll go inside soon."

Her mind raced with each passing second, her imagination in overdrive. She fought the temptation to take another look.

Seeing Wade touching someone else was hard enough. If she caught him hugging or kissing her—well, she didn't know if she could handle it.

The spot on her cheek where Wade had kissed her tingled, and she grazed the tips of her fingers across her skin. What had that been about? An impulse? A goodbye? A decision to do something sweet before rushing headfirst into danger to protect her?

Each possible explanation made the blood in her head pulse louder.

She shook away her fascination with the simple gesture. It didn't matter why he'd done it. It was clear the peck on her cheek didn't mean a damn thing. He hadn't wasted any time wrapping his arms around another woman as soon as she presented herself.

"Jude!"

She blew out a long breath and stood. He couldn't see how much he affected her—couldn't know how he could still completely shake her world with something so dang little and obviously meaningless. Besides, she couldn't get sucked into his vortex. Not now. Not ever.

"Everything's okay. You can come out."

Determined to play it cool, she set Macey on the ground and led her to Wade.

Wrigley galloped toward her.

"Sorry 'bout that," Wade said, scratching the back of his neck. "Summer's a friend. She was worried when I didn't open the bar."

Jude pressed her lips together and shrugged. "Nice friend. Your dog's freezing. We should head back to the apartment."

He nodded and stayed a step behind her as she marched back up the deck steps and rushed inside. She wished she could slam closed the sliding glass door and keep Wade outside. Too much turmoil bubbled in her stomach. She couldn't keep it down much longer before she exploded pent-up emotion all over him and anyone else who happened to be around.

Her phone vibrated in her pocket just as Wade's phone rang.

She secured her device and a dozen text messages littered her screen—all from Matthew and one from Brandon.

"Hey, Cruz," Wade said, answering the phone as he slid the door closed. "What's up?"

She listened to Wade as she opened her messages. Her heart fell to the floor. Wade's words became garbled in her ears, his expression pinched with concern. Bile slid up her throat as she clicked through the messages, each more alarming than the last.

"Jude, Jude!" Wade's hands were on her arms, his face right in front of hers. "What's wrong?"

Her grip loosened on her phone as she let her arm drop and dangle at her side. "Matthew. He hurt Matthew. He hurt my brother."

"I know."

She blinked, bringing Wade into focus. "You know? How do you know? I can't—" A sob caught in her throat, and she pitched forward.

Wade opened his arms and she fell against him. "That was Cruz on the phone. He's at the hospital now. Matthew's in surgery. Brandon found him unconscious in the living room when he got home. He didn't have a ton of details, but the video feed from their doorbell confirmed it was Benji Blitz."

"I need to get to the hospital. Now. I need to make sure he's okay." She buried her head in his chest. Tears spilled from her eyes.

Resting his chin on the top of her head, he tightened his hold. "I don't know if that's a good idea."

She pulled away, anger flaring hot in her chest. "I'm not

asking your permission. My brother is in the hospital. I need to go see him. I told him I'd visit him once everything was all cleared up. Once it was safe. I put him off time and time again, always with some excuse about how I couldn't come back. And now he's hurt and it's my fault. I brought the danger to town. Sent the bad guy to his door."

"You couldn't have known he'd go after Matthew."

Her bottom lip trembled. "I should have guessed. He went to my parents' house. Talked to my mom. If he found them, Matthew wouldn't have been too difficult to find."

Wade frowned. "How do you know this guy went to your parents' home?"

Ashamed she hadn't thought to be insistent that Matthew stay safe and on alert, she dropped her gaze to the floor. "Matthew told me. Mom called him and was freaking out. She got the same story you did—a detective was in search of me. No other details. I told Matthew I was safe and not to worry. This is my fault. If I'd have told you or Cruz, someone could have done something to protect him."

He reached for her.

She shook her head and took a step backward. "I have to see him."

"It's not safe. Matthew might live in Elm Ridge, but there's only one county hospital. Benji might be watching—waiting for you to show up. Putting yourself in danger won't do Matthew any good."

His words made sense, but she wouldn't be swayed. "You don't understand. I haven't seen my brother in twelve years. If he dies before I get a chance to make things right, I'll never forgive myself." Her voice cracked as years of regret slammed against her like a raging river.

Wade scrubbed a palm over his face. "Let me call Cruz."

She lifted a shoulder and sniffed back her tears. "Go ahead. But if you won't take me, I'll find another way."

"Trust me, the last thing I want is to tell you what to do. I know you won't listen anyway." He smirked, as if remembering a million times she'd done the exact opposite of what he'd wanted. "But if I take you to see Matthew, I want to be smart about it and Cruz will have a better understanding of how to do that."

"Fine," she said. "Call. I'll be ready to go as soon as you get off the phone." She said it with way more confidence than she felt. Because when it came to seeing any member of her family, she wasn't sure if she'd ever really be ready.

ANXIETY KNOTTED Wade's stomach as he maneuvered Chet's truck into the employee's parking lot behind the county hospital. He was grateful his buddy was fine with swapping trucks for the afternoon—an added layer of protection against being spotted—but the anxiousness coursing through his veins wouldn't leave until he had Jude far away from the hospital.

The stakes were too high, the possibility an ambush waited for Jude too prevalent in his mind.

Shutting off the engine, he hooked an arm over the back of the seat and let the tips of his fingers rest on Jude's shoulder. "You ready?"

She bit her thumbnail and stared out the windshield. "Yes. No. Maybe. Hell, this is terrifying, but I know I need to be here."

He nodded, understanding the desire to be by a loved one's side when they were injured and scared. "Cruz is waiting outside the break room. He positioned several unmarked police cars around the perimeter to keep an eye out for anything unusual, as well as plain-clothed officers inside."

She flipped down the visor and wiped tears from her face. Not like it helped.

Her red, puffy eyes made his heart lurch. Dropping his arm, he took hold of her hand, forcing her nubby nail from her mouth. Her fear was evident, but he understood her panic went much deeper than the external threat on her life. "I'm right beside you. Whenever you want to leave, just say the word."

"Okay," she said, blowing out a long breath. "I'm ready."

He grabbed the bag she'd brought along and hurried out of the truck to open her door. He had a sneaking suspicion one of the reasons Cruz had been on board with Jude visiting the hospital was her willingness to bring the photos. She'd balked at the idea of speaking with the Mill Harbor police, and it hadn't been the right time to press the issue, but she was more than happy to part ways with the pictures that had landed her in this mess to begin with.

She climbed down and sought out his hand, holding on tight.

Her palm nestled into his like a puzzle piece. A piece that had been missing for way too long. But he couldn't think too much of the gesture. She was scared and wanted some comfort. That's all. He'd give her what she needed and do them both a huge favor by not reading into it more than he should.

A car door slammed, snapping him back to the moment. He glanced over his shoulder and noted a middle-aged woman in a puffy coat and green scrubs walking across the parking lot, her attention fixed on her phone.

He gave Jude's hand a gentle squeeze. "We should hurry and get inside." Ducking his chin against the wind, he led Jude through the employee's entrance. He nodded hello to a handful of nurses who gathered for a quick moment to grab some coffee or get off their feet for a few minutes.

Jude stayed close behind him. The bill of her hat was pulled low over her face. She kept her head down, turned away from the curious eyes that followed them as he led them out the door.

Cruz stood across the hall. His face grim, his stance rigid.

Jude dropped Wade's hand and rushed forward. "How's Matthew? Can I see him?"

Wade wiped his palm on his jeans and stood by Jude's side.

"Last I heard he was still in surgery," Cruz said.

"How bad was it? What exactly happened?" Jude asked, panic lacing through her voice.

Cruz laid a hand on her elbow and turned her toward a small room behind him. "Let's step inside and talk."

Wade glanced at the name plate beside the door before following them and closing the door. "Nice of Frank to give up his office for a little bit."

"Go ahead and take a seat." Cruz gestured to the chairs across from the large oak desk.

Jude shook her head. "I can't sit now. I need to know what happened. I know Matthew was attacked in his home, but I want details."

Cruz winced. "The details aren't pretty, and really, all we know are the injuries your brother sustained and who inflicted those injuries. Benji Blitz went to his apartment, but there's no audio on the doorbell camera so we can't be sure what was said. A minute or two passes before Benji punches Matthew and pushes him inside. Brandon found him twenty minutes after Benji left. Beaten pretty badly."

Jude squeezed her eyes shut. "Matthew knew the man had hurt me. He wouldn't have just stood there and had a conversation with him. He would have wanted to defend me anyway he could."

"Your brother loves you," Wade said.

Sniffing, she nodded and opened her eyes. "I love him, too. I need to see him and tell him."

"I understand, but that can't happen until he's out of surgery. Chances are he'll be taken to the ICU, and we'll need to know what the stipulations are for visitors."

"Brandon will let me see him," she said, her words wobbly.

Cruz offered her a small smile. "I'm sure he will, when the time comes. But while we wait, can I see the pictures again? Wade said you're willing to let me show them to the police in Mill Harbor."

Wade handed over the bag he'd looped over his shoulder.

"Thanks," she said, digging inside to grab the memory card. "Take this. I don't want anything to do with it."

Cruz accepted the small memory card that had done so much damage. "And what about speaking with the detective in charge of the case? I can assure you they don't think you've done anything wrong."

"She's not ready for that," Wade said, reading the tortured expression on her face. "And now's not the time to talk about it further. Not with Matthew in surgery."

She offered him grateful smile. "Thank you."

"I understand," Cruz said, raising his palms. "I'll handle all communication with Mill Harbor PD. You've done plenty. Now do you want to wait—"

A rough knock sounded at the door before it swung open. Jenson Metcalf stormed inside. He opened his mouth, but before anything came out, his gaze landed on Jude.

Jude shrunk against Wade and knotted her hands in front of her. Her body went rigid, her gaze instantly landing on the floor.

Picking up on the shift of energy, Wade worked his jaw back and forth and positioned himself between Jude and her father. "Mr. Metcalf," he said.

Jenson's stare turned to stone for a brief second before he softened his features and grinned. "Jude Bug! You're home!"

11

The familiar punch of cologne that rolled off her father made Jude's stomach heave. She reached for Wade, needing an anchor to steady her so she didn't fall to the floor. Coming here to see Matthew meant the risk of running into her family was high, but she hadn't been prepared for her dad to barge into what she'd thought was a safe space.

Wade steadied her with a hand on the small of her back, his other arm rigid under her death grip.

Her dad's fake grin melted into concern, predatory green eyes rounded and mouth turned down ever so slightly at the corners. "I can't believe it's really you. It's been so long since we've seen you—since we talked to you. Your mother will be so happy to see you. Especially with everything going on."

He took a step forward and she flinched, pushing closer to Wade. Her mouth went dry.

A flash of anger took over Jenson's face before he schooled his features. He held open his arms. "Well, come here and give your old man a hug. It's been one hell of a day. Seeing you will make things just a little bit better."

She needed to say something, do something other than stand in the room, tension thick and uncomfortable, staring at her dad.

Keeping his hand firmly planted on her back, Wade side-stepped Jude so he was a few inches in front of her. "So sorry to hear about Matthew, sir."

Jenson dropped his arms and cut his gaze to Wade. "Thank you. We're all pretty shaken. As you can imagine, we have a lot of questions."

Jude fought not to squirm. She wasn't stupid. The questions were meant for her. Chances were Matthew wasn't even a concern for her dad, even with his life in the balance. He'd made it perfectly clear Matthew's life choices weren't okay for the Metcalf family but thank God her brother had thumbed his nose at their father's judgement—choosing Brandon even if it cost him more than it ever should have.

Cruz cleared his throat, drawing eyes his way. "We all have questions, Mayor. And I can assure you I won't stop until I have them answered. Why don't we step outside? I can brief you on what I know so far."

A vein ticked at Jenson's temple, a sign he was losing his patience.

I'm okay. He can't touch me. Can't torture me or hurt me. Not anymore.

Jenson gave a curt nod then fixed another smile on her. "So glad to see you, Jude Bug. Can't wait to catch up."

Cruz ushered him out to the hall, closing the door behind him.

Her knees buckled and she fell against Wade's hard chest. Dark spots invaded her vision. She closed her eyes, but it just increased the sense of panic clawing at her throat.

"Hey. I got ya, darlin'. Let's get you in this chair real quick. Nice and easy."

She leaned most of her weight on his strong arms as he helped lower her onto the chair. Sweat coated her palms. She wiped them up and down the rough material of her jeans, rubbing her thighs again and again and again as memories slapped her. Her chest tightened, her breaths caught in the web of fear wedged in her throat. She struggled to take in air, and tears stung the corners of her eyes.

Wade crouched in front of her. "Look at me, honey."

His voice was distant, jumbled as if he projected his words through a puddle of mud. But she latched onto it, focused on the thick, southern drawl and obvious concern. She blinked, pulling herself from the abyss she'd withdrawn into countless times as a child.

She wasn't that child any longer. She was strong and capable and had spent countless hours—and dollars—working on herself. On wading through the bullshit tossed at her from her father so she'd never have to come back to this dark place in her mind for survival.

Blinking, she stared into Wade's brown eyes. Concentrated on the feel of his hand on hers. The scent of pine and sandal-wood with a hint of citrus that clung to his skin. The pressure in her chest lessened, her breathing evened out and her vision cleared. Tears leaked over her cheeks, and she dashed them away, angry that all it had taken was one brief encounter with her dad to reduce her to a puddle of fear and panic.

Just like when she was a kid.

"There you go," Wade said. "Take a second and catch your breath."

She licked her dry lips and finally stopped the motion of her palms against her thighs. Heat crashed against her cheeks. "I'm sorry you had to see that," she said, dropping her gaze to the floor.

"You have nothing to apologize for," Wade said. A beat of

awkward silence simmered in the air before he continued. "Wanna talk about it?"

She wiped her face then ran a palm over her hair, as if righting her appearance would right everything else in the world. A stupid Metcalf family habit she'd never outgrown—look the part, play the part, act the part.

But she was tired of pretending. Tired of acting like everything was okay because she'd left everyone who'd hurt her behind. If nothing else, running into her dad had shown her that she hadn't healed as much as she'd thought. Maybe running—putting years and distance between them wasn't the answer. Hell, even therapy hadn't helped. Maybe it was time to do the one thing she'd always feared the most.

Open up to the one man whose opinion mattered the most to her.

Sucking in a deep breath, she took hold of Wade's hands and nodded. "Yes. I do want to talk about it, but not right now. Right now I want to focus all of my energy on Matthew, maybe even try to find Brandon so I can be there for him, and then we can have a conversation tonight. A real, honest to goodness conversation where I finally lay all my cards on the table."

"I'd like that."

A different kind of fear twisted her stomach. One that told her if Wade doubted her words—doubted her truth—it might be the one thing to finally break her.

The door swung open and a tall young woman with sandy blond hair and red-rimmed eyes popped her head inside. "Dad? Are you still—"

Jude's gaze latched onto her baby sister, and she slowly rose on shaky legs. "Laura? Is that you?" Gone was the gangly freckled-faced girl she'd left behind, in her place a stunning young woman with shoulder length hair and flawless skin.

Except the tiny twinge of a bruise her makeup couldn't quite hide.

Laura's mouth fell open for a second before she snapped it shut. Fire blazed from her cobalt eyes. "I don't know what you're doing here but you can go right back to hell where you belong."

The door slammed shut, echoing the sound of Jude's shattering heart.

⁓

WADE STARED at the closed door, unsure of his next move. In the last five minutes, he'd gotten a crash course in the Metcalf family dynamics. A course he never wanted to take and, to be honest, had his head spinning.

"Was that really my sister?" Jude asked, astonishment in her hollow voice.

He stood, hating the ashen pallor of her skin. She'd come face-to-face with two people from her past who she hadn't spoken with in twelve long years. And from his understanding, at least one of those people didn't deserve to be within three feet of Jude. But he'd get into the specifics of her reaction to Jenson later.

"Yes, that was Laura. She's grown up a lot since the last time you saw her."

Jude snorted. "I'd say. I don't know if I'd have recognized her if I'd passed her on the street. Did you see the bruise?" She pinched the bridge of her nose and paced across the small room. "I left to protect her. And she's covering bruises with makeup? Did he escalate after I left?"

He strained to hear the words she mumbled under her breath. Dread settled into the pit of his stomach. "I saw the bruises."

She stopped and spun to face him. "If he hit her. If he touched her..."

The dread turned to stone-cold anger. Her insinuation

fisted his hands at his sides. Her initial thought of who hurt her sister was bad enough, but the truth of Laura's circumstances wasn't any better. "Bruises aren't uncommon on Laura. People have tried to help her, but there's nothing anyone can do until she makes the choice to help herself."

Jude frowned, head cocked to the side. "Help herself? What do you mean?"

"Laura lives with her boyfriend, Isaac Heck. You know him?" Just saying the man's name boiled his blood. Everyone in town knew what an asshole Isaac was, but unless Laura chose to press charges for the abuse he inflicted, there wasn't much anyone could do. Besides plot ways to beat the shit out of him and teach him a lesson.

Jude wrinkled her nose. "The kid who lived down the street? The one who used to take a bat to all the mailboxes?"

"That's the one. He and Laura have an apartment in town. He's in college but works for your dad at city hall. He's a real piece of work."

"I can't believe this. I wanted to protect her but instead I left an innocent girl in shark infested waters. I wish she'd ask someone for help."

"I wish you would have asked for help," Wade said.

Tears welled up in her eyes, but she bit her top lip to keep them at bay.

Cruz swept back inside, interrupting the moment.

Wade couldn't tell if he was relieved or not. He wanted to know what Jude went through, wanted her to trust him enough to share every last sordid detail, but his world was spinning around him. If he was going to be there for Jude when she finally bared her soul, he had to get a freaking grip. Because as horrible as he felt, none of that mattered. This wasn't about him. It was about Jude, and he needed to be strong for her.

"Your brother is out of surgery, and they were able to take

him to a private room. I spoke with Brandon, and he said to come on down. He'll make sure you see him first."

"What about my dad?" she asked, her voice small. "Did Brandon send for him too?"

Cruz shook his head. "No. I told your dad to go to the waiting room with the rest of your family. Brandon thought you'd want some time with Matthew on your own."

Jude finally cracked a small smile.

Appreciation tightened Wade's chest. He didn't know Brandon well, but he'd always liked the guy. After giving so much consideration to Jude, he just went up a few notches in his book.

"I'll walk with you, if that's okay?" Cruz asked.

"Yes, I'd appreciate that," Jude said.

Wade took hold of her hand and walked beside her as they followed Cruz down the hall. He kept her close, staying on the lookout for any possible threats. Staff hurried passed him, and clusters of visitors gathered by open doors. The familiar punch of bleach and sickness tightened his grip on Jude. Her demons might be the ones waiting to attack, but his own lingered in the shadows. And being in the hospital where he'd spent way too much time recently brought them a step closer to the light.

"Hey, Wade. How's your mom?" Dr. Bailey, his mom's primary care physician, waved from beside the nurses' station, as if he'd conjured her with his thoughts.

"Hiya, Doc. She's good." He tucked his lips and dipped his chin before turning in the opposite direction.

He cast Jude a quick glance, but she kept her head down and didn't appear to register the greeting by the doctor who knew his mom way too well.

Cruz stopped beside a closed door. "Here we are. I'll wait outside for you to finish then walk you back to your vehicle."

She hovered her fist an inch from the door then glanced up at Wade. "Will you come in with me?"

"Whatever you want."

She knocked.

The door swept open. Brandon stood just inside the room, worry aging him years since the last time Wade had seen him.

A sob broke from his lips and he gathered Jude into a hug, breaking Wade's connection to her. "It's so good to see you."

"I'm sorry. I'm so, so sorry," Jude stammered.

Brandon pulled back and wiped her face with the pad of his thumb. "You haven't done anything wrong, and Matthew will be so damn happy to see you. He's going to be fine. Doctors expect a full recovery. He's still asleep, but talk to him. Let him know you're here. Give him something to look forward to."

She nodded. "I will."

"I'll head out to talk to your parents. Give them an update. That should give you a few minutes alone."

"Thank you."

Brandon and Cruz left the room together, Brandon disappearing down the hall while Cruz stood just outside the room with his back to them.

Jude recaptured Wade's hand and drew in a shuddering breath.

Beeping machines and fluorescent lights filled the space. He stepped beside Jude, approaching the bed.

"Oh my God," she said and covered her mouth.

Wade swallowed hard. Bruises and swelling covered Matthew's face, making it almost impossible to recognize him. An IV pumped bags of medicine into his body. A cast swallowed his left arm.

Jude dropped her palm from her mouth and covered Matthew's arm. "I'm here, big brother. I'll be here whenever you wake up. I'm not going anywhere."

The statement was like balm to Wade's soul, but he couldn't read too much into it. He couldn't count on Jude staying in town.

"Wade?" she asked, her gaze fixed on her brother.

"Yes?"

"Tell Cruz I'll speak with anyone he needs me to. Do anything I can to catch the bastard who did this. This asshole needs to pay."

12

Trudging into the apartment, all Jude wanted to do was close her eyes and forget everything that had happened the last couple of days. Matthew hadn't woken up from his medically-induced coma, but no way her father would be put off much longer. And she couldn't handle another encounter with him—or her mom and Laura.

So like the coward she was, she'd left the hospital.

Macey pranced at Wade's feet, and he grabbed a leash and snapped it on her collar. "She needs to go to the bathroom. I'll be quick."

Jude forced a small smile and nodded.

He hurried outside at the same moment Mia came to the door with her arms full of shopping bags. They exchanged a brief greeting before Mia bustled inside.

"Hey," Mia said. "I talked to Chet. I'm so sorry about your brother. I'll just drop this stuff off then get out of your hair."

"Mia! What did you do?" Jude asked, rushing to help her friend unload her burdens. "I only needed a few things."

Mia shrugged and struggled to make it to the table before spilling her haul on the floor. "I got everything on the list and a few other things I thought you might like. I also stopped by my restaurant and grabbed some food. With everything going on, I figured neither you nor Wade would want to cook. I wasn't sure what you like to eat, so I brought enough house favorites to feed five."

Gratitude chased away some of the gloominess that had followed her home from the hospital. For the past twelve years, she'd been on her own. Depended on herself and no one else. Having someone—a brand new friend at that—step up and take care of her was something she'd yearned for.

"Thank you," she said, choking out the words.

Mia flashed a smile and started unpacking the bags. "No problem. I picked up some groceries too. You're all set for at least a week."

Jude got started putting away the groceries. A plastic sack from the drugstore caught her attention and she pulled out a box of hair dye. "What's this?"

Mia grinned. "You mentioned earlier how much you hate the pink hair. And honestly, it doesn't make much sense to keep it that shade since the guy after you knows so much about you. And if he's caught a glimpse of you at all since you've been in town, he knows it's pink. Not to mention you don't plan on leaving this place anyway. I thought you might want to go back to your natural color."

Hugging the box to her chest, Jude let out a long sigh. "I know it sounds crazy, but I feel like this might bring back a tiny piece of normalcy to my life."

"That doesn't sound crazy at all," Mia said, unloading white Styrofoam boxes that smelled like heaven and placing them on the counter. "Besides, I've always heard blonds have more fun."

Jude snorted. "I'm not sure about that."

With the food all packed away, except the meal Mia had brought which stayed on the counter, Mia scooped up the last two bags and dangled them from her forearm. "How about I take these new clothes with me? I'll put them through the wash really quick."

"Are you sure? You've already done too much."

"Positive. Do you have anything else I can add to the laundry?"

Jude hurried to her backpack and pulled out the clothes she'd worn the day before and handed them over. "You're an angel."

"Tell Chet that, won't ya?" Mia shot her a wink and headed for the door. "Lock this behind me. Wade has a key on him. He's still right out front, but better to be safe."

As the door shut, Jude studied the box of hair dye. The color was almost a perfect match to her natural hue. A lightness swept over her, and she ran to the bathroom. She didn't care if it seemed weird or ridiculous to do something so frivolous, she was doing something for her—something to bring back a little piece of herself she'd left behind.

With expert hands—she'd colored her own hair too many times to count in pursuit of self-discovery and expression over the years—she unpacked the supplies and got started threading the pungent dye through her long strands. The meticulous work kept her glove-covered hands and mind busy, for a brief moment allowing her to escape the heaviness weighing her down. Right now, she was just a woman who needed to color her hair.

A soft knock sounded on the door. "Jude? Is everything all right in there?"

The wariness in Wade's voice lifted her lips, and a foreign giddiness set off her nerves. And these nerves had nothing to do with the danger tracking her down and everything to do with hoping a boy she had no right pining for thought she'd look pretty after making a drastic change.

She rolled her eyes. She was being silly. Dying her hair back to blond was for her pleasure and no one else's. What Wade thought shouldn't matter one bit.

"I'm fine. About to jump in the shower. I'll be out in a little while." She studied her smothered locks, debating on if she should rinse the chemicals out and leave it wet or actually put a little work into her hair.

She opened the cabinet and found a hair dryer and curling iron. Clearly she should do more than rinse and let it air dry. Just so she could make sure she liked the color and nothing more.

"Are you hungry at all?" Wade asked, drawing her attention back to him.

The thought of eating made her wrinkle her nose. "Not really, but I suppose I should eat something. Mia left food on the counter."

Wade chuckled, the sound warm and soothing through the thin door. "Hard to miss that. Once I hear the shower turn off, I'll set everything out. Take your time."

Grinning, she twisted the knobs in the tub until she found the perfect water temperature. She undressed, careful to lay out her clothes so they wouldn't get wet, then stepped under the warm spray of water. Lifting her arms, she worked her hands through her hair, making sure to rinse out all the dye. Slivers of chemicals and miscolored water circled the drain. The vise squeezing her lungs loosened by a fraction, allowing herself to finally pull in a full breath.

She had a long way to go to find herself again, but she'd finally taken the first small step.

The scents of garlic and parmesan floated from the covered dishes Wade had set on the table, combining with the odd smell coming from the bathroom. He'd wanted to ask Jude what hell was going on in there, but the question was more than a little invasive.

He glanced at his watch, and his stomach growled. Not

quite 4:00 pm, even though he swore that couldn't be right. The amount of stress and anxiety heaped on his shoulders, making his body ache as though he'd been the one physically assaulted, made it seem like the hour should be much later. Add to that he hadn't eaten more than a protein bar, and he was tempted to shovel food on his plate and dig in.

He glanced at his watch a second time, as if checking the time would hurry Jude. He'd waited for the water to stop in the bathroom before preparing the meal. Okay, not preparing, more like displaying. He'd set the small, round table with plates and silverware, filling two glasses with water. He'd scooped the chicken alfredo into a white dish and covered it to keep it warm, then heated up the garlic bread Mia made from scratch in the oven.

He'd elected to put the rest of the food she'd brought in the fridge. He knew Jude would eat chicken alfredo whether she was hungry or not, and the rest of the food would keep for another day or two.

The sound of a creaking door turned him toward the bathroom, and his jaw dropped.

Jude stood with a wicked smile on her make-up free face, her long, blond hair flowing around her shoulders in luxurious curls he'd do anything to run his fingers through.

He rose, hand over his heart, and words evaded him. She looked so much more like the girl he used to know with her natural color back. Memories he'd held at bay finally broke down the dam and poured over him.

She twirled a long piece of hair around her index finger and rubbed her bare foot over her calf. "Do you like it?"

With words still not coming, he nodded.

"Well...say something," she said, a laugh catching in her throat.

He coughed, clearing his airways. "You're beautiful. I mean, you were with the pink hair too, but this...this is you."

The wickedness vanished from her grin, replaced with an almost shy quality that made her look so damn vulnerable. "I agree. I mean, not with the beautiful part." She batted a hand through the air as if that were ludicrous. "But being more me. Mia picked up the color when she went shopping. I couldn't resist."

"I'm glad you didn't." He couldn't keep his eyes off her, his mind from straying as pictures flickered in his brain like a black and white home video.

She leaned to the side as if to look around him. "What's all that?"

"Oh," he said, suddenly remembering the meal and how hungry he was. "One of the many meals Mia brought over was Chicken Alfredo. I hope it's okay that's what I set out for us. If not, there's a casserole of some kind and a chicken pot pie and some homemade soup. I can heat up whatever you like."

Her eyes lit and she crossed over to the table. "This is perfect and smells amazing."

He bit back a sigh of relief. *Stop rambling on and acting like this is the first time you've seen a beautiful woman—first time you've spent time alone with Jude.*

Macey darted from her spot on the couch and pranced around Jude's legs.

Laughing, Jude gave her a pat on the head. "Sorry, girl. I don't share my food."

He chuckled and took a seat as she settled into the chair across from him. Leaning forward, he snatched up her plate and filled it with pasta then added a slice of bread before handing it over. "Do you need anything else?"

Typically, he'd offer wine with a meal like this, maybe even light a candle or two, but this wasn't a date. And after all the affection they'd given each other over the course of a very stressful day, he had to keep some boundaries in place. Even if he didn't want to.

Shaking her head, she waited for him to fill his own plate before spearing a piece of chicken and slipping it into her mouth. "Oh. My. God," she moaned.

He tightened his jaw to keep his mouth from falling open and focused on taking his own bite. His thoughts echoed Jude's sentiment, but he kept them to himself.

"Mia said she got this from her restaurant," Jude said. "How long has that been around?"

"Not long. A few months at most. But the place is always busy." He hadn't made it to Homespun as much as he'd have liked, but whenever he managed to grab a meal there, he was always impressed.

Jude frowned. "Has that created any issues with the Chill N' Grill? I mean, the town's not that big. Does having another restaurant cut into your profits?"

He shook his head and took a bite of warm bread. "Not really. We've got plenty of people around to share, and Mia's done a hell of a job. Everyone loves her and her food. But my customers are loyal, not to mention we serve alcohol."

She dropped her head, gaze fixed on the food on her plate.

"What is it?" The energy had shifted, and he was tired of pretending everything was okay. Of not asking the hard questions because he didn't want to have an uncomfortable conversation. Yes, he'd been young when he'd been with Jude, but by not diving in and finding out what was really going on in her life, he'd lost her.

Setting down her fork, she blew out a long breath and finally met his eye. "You're right. Loyalty to that restaurant runs pretty damn deep. It's the reason I left this town all by myself instead of with the man I loved."

Her words hit him like a sucker punch to the gut. A tornado of resentment and sadness and confusion whipped to life inside him. Tonight was supposed to be about being there for

Jude while she told him why she'd left, not making him feel like shit because of the choice he'd made.

A choice he'd make again in a heartbeat. Because if he hadn't stayed, where would his family's legacy be? Where would his mother be?

She'd be alone with no memories, no future, and no one to see to her every need. And he wouldn't let Jude make him feel bad, not when she refused to tell him why she'd had to run that night. Refused to let him all the way in and see the hurt and damage that was there. So before he could trust her enough to tell her what happened after she'd skipped town and left him broken hearted, he needed to understand what had pushed her over the edge.

He shoved his plate aside and looked her dead in the eye. He didn't want there to be one ounce of doubt about what he meant. What he needed. "Loyalty's one of those things that only works when it goes both ways. You left me. Left me a broken mess while I grieved for my father and looked after my mother. Left me when the whole world had been dumped on my shoulders, and I didn't even know which way was up."

She dropped her gaze and shifted in her seat.

He gritted his teeth and fought to keep his composure. Making her uncomfortable was the last thing he wanted, but he had to press on. Needed her to see what losing her had done to him. "So you're right, I guess. Loyalty cost you me, but it wasn't because I wouldn't have given my right arm to help you out of any trouble. Hell, you didn't ask for help, didn't trust me enough to tell me there was trouble. And maybe a part of that's on me—on things I should have seen—but I was just a kid trying the best I knew how."

She finally lifted her gaze to meet his. "I did trust you. I always have. What I went through..." She lifted her shoulders. "I didn't know how to tell anyone. Was too scared to try."

His heart lurched, and he lifted a palm. "I don't want to

diminish your pain—your trauma. I just need you to understand mine. If you want to sit there and act like I pushed you
away and didn't choose you, you're only fooling yourself.
Because I would have chosen you every single day. But you
weren't loyal enough to let me all the way in. To stand by *my*
side when I needed you more than I needed air. So if you want
to hash this out, darlin, you better start talking."

13

The thick, creamy sauce turned to stone in the pit of Jude's stomach. She'd promised Wade she'd tell him everything tonight, but why had she opened her big mouth and started the conversation off in the worst way possible?

Yes, she knew Wade was grieving when she'd asked him to leave town with her, but she was so fixated on getting the hell out of a dodge, she'd seen his refusal as nothing other than flat out rejection. She'd imaged a new life where they could move on from their hurt and pain and create a brighter future.

Instead, she'd left with a broken heart and a shattered soul without giving Wade's needs a second thought.

She squared her shoulders and folded her hands in her lap. Her heart pounded like crazy, and a subtle buzzing rang in her ears. "You're right. I didn't think about helping you cope with the loss of your dad," she said, running a hand through her hair as frustration knotted her nerves. "I thought about what I needed, and what I would need if I were you. That meant leaving Pine Valley and getting away from our troubles."

Wade scrubbed a palm over his face as if he wasn't sure if he was ready for this conversation. "You wrecked me when you left. But my mom needed me. She was a mess after Dad died. I couldn't abandon her. Leave her alone to run the Chill N' Grill by herself when she was struggling to just put one foot in front of the other."

Guilt twisted her insides. "I never wanted you to abandon your mom."

"Are you sure about that? You had no problem abandoning your own mother."

She winced and dropped her gaze to her half-filled plate.

"I'm sorry," Wade said. "I shouldn't have said that. If today showed me anything, it's that I had no idea what you were going through at home."

She tightened her grip on her intwined hands, afraid to meet his gaze. "I deserved it. You're right. I haven't spoken with or seen my mom since I left, and I have my reasons for that. But I shouldn't expect you to understand those reasons if I never explained them."

"Will you?" Wade asked, voice low and husky. "I want to know. I want to understand."

Sighing, she finally met his gaze. "I left because of my dad."

He tightened his jaw, eyes hard. "I figured that part out today."

A sad smile lifted the corner of her mouth. "I used to be better at hiding how he made me feel. I think being gone for so long, then blindsided when he showed up when I was already so emotionally raw, made it impossible to put on the mask he demanded we all wore. Made it impossible to paste on a smile and pretend he wasn't a monster."

"You've been through a lot the last couple of days. The fact you've kept any semblance of composure is remarkable."

She huffed out a humorless laugh. "I was a trembling mess when he walked into that office."

"You are strong. You are anything but a mess."

"I'm a coward." Tears tunneled her vision. "I was weak, and I left nothing but pain behind me. Pain I might've stopped if I would have stayed."

Wade moved to his feet and fell to his knees at her side. He cradled her hands in his. "Hey now. No tears and definitely no coming down so hard on yourself. Just talk to me."

She sniffed, but it did nothing to vanquish the moisture from spilling over her lashes. "I couldn't take it anymore. I couldn't be in that house. Never knowing what kind of mood he'd be in—if he'd shower me with love and affection or treat me like the scum under his shoe."

Wade squeezed her hand. "I'm sorry you had to go through that. I wish you would have told me."

She lifted a shoulder. "I was afraid to tell anyone. If Dad ever saw me act out or got wind of me speaking in a way he didn't approve, he'd not only take it out on me. He'd take it out on Laura."

"What do you mean?" Wade asked, frowning.

She squeezed her eyes closed for a beat, hating going back to all the bad memories. A light tug on her arm opened her eyes and lifted her to her feet. She found herself standing in front of Wade, their hands still twined together.

"Let's take a seat somewhere more comfortable. I'll clean up later," Wade said then led her to the worn-in couch.

She settled into the corner, hooking her leg up and shifting to face him. Macey jumped into her lap. A chill swept over Jude, and she crossed her arms over her chest, rubbing her fingers up and down her long-sleeved t-shirt to warm up. But the chill had nothing to do with the temperature.

"You were saying?" He prompted, eyes wide and filled with concern.

She swallowed the bile creeping up her throat. "Dad's biggest concern is his image. And as the mayor, people were always watching us. Always measuring what we said and how we acted, and if something slipped out that shouldn't—or God forbid I reacted to him like I did earlier today—he'd make sure I paid."

Wade's Adam's apple bopped, a sure sign he struggled to keep his temper from showing. "Paid how? Did he hit you?"

She shook her head. "He never touched us. It was more like emotional warfare. He'd take things away or hide them. Things I needed or loved, not like punishing a petulant child by taking away screen time. I mean stashing my homework so I'd get a bad grade or making me think my cat had run away because I'd misbehaved when really he'd locked it in the basement."

Stroking Macey's silky fur, she let herself go back to the dark days she tried so hard to forget. But in order for Wade to understand what she'd survived, she needed to show him what she'd escaped. "As I got older, the punishments got worse. Instead of hiding my homework, he'd hide Laura's. Instead of my cat being locked in the basement, I was."

The gut-wrenching sensation of being confined in the dark basement overtook her. Her teeth chattered and pulse pounded against her temple. She focused on Macey's soft fur and avoided the pity coming off Wade in waves. "Once he realized it was more upsetting for him to punish my sister for my actions, he took it ever further. Cutting her hair inch by inch if he didn't like my attitude, forcing her to sit at the table and eat food she hated—like dill pickles or spoonfuls of mustard—if I disobeyed. Locking her in the closet in the laundry room if I spoke out of turn. Every move I made was scrutinized, every action seemingly leading to another slap on the wrist for me— and an even bigger one for Laura. I thought if I left, he'd leave her alone."

"Why didn't you ever tell anyone? Hell, why didn't you ever tell me? My parents loved you like their own. They would have stepped in. Would have done whatever they could to help."

She snorted, wishing she still had some of his naiveté.

Some of his innocence. "Who'd believe the word of a kid who lived in a pretty blue house with a white picket fence and parents who portrayed nothing but love and kindness? I wore the nicest clothes, was always well-behaved, and never carried a mark from anything other than my own clumsiness. Nobody can see invisible scars, and no one would ever believe a child over a powerful and respected man like my father."

~

ANGER COURSED through Wade's veins. Anger at what Jude had been put through for so long, and anger at himself for not seeing it.

He couldn't do anything to help the girl who was too scared to speak out, but he could do something now. "I would have believed you, and I have a feeling more people would have taken your side than you thought. I never liked your dad. There have to be others in town who've seen him for who he really is."

"You believe me now because you saw my reaction earlier. And you didn't like my dad because he was your girlfriend's father. He was always tough on you." She offered him a weak, watery smile.

Leaning forward, he hooked an arm around her shoulders. "I haven't been Jenson Metcalf's daughter's boyfriend in a long time. I didn't like him before, I hate the bastard after hearing all this. But even without you telling me what a monster he is, I've seen chips in his smooth veneer. He's always putting on a show. Always trying to win votes and kiss babies. People can only wear a mask for so long before it slips. Even your dad."

She shivered and sandwiched her top lip between her teeth as though she didn't quite believe him. "I suppose you're right, but back then, that seemed impossible."

He hated asking the question that had plagued him all day,

but he couldn't hold back any longer. "What about your mom? Did she know what was happening?"

Jude tightened her jaw and dropped her gaze. She strummed her fingertips over Macy's back. "She knew."

Conflicting emotions battled inside him. His memories of Nicole Metcalf were of a nice woman with a pleasant smile and caring demeanor. He couldn't align the woman he'd known most of his life with a mother who allowed her children to be abused.

"Ahhh," Jude said, throwing her head back and pressing the heels of her hands over her eyes. "This is a lot for me to talk about. My dad is less complicated for me to wrap my mind around at this point in my life. He's a toxic asshole I have no desire to have a relationship with. I had to shed him from my life like a snake shedding its skin. But my mom?" Her voice cracked and she curled into a ball, as if trying to disappear. "I just wanted her to stand up for me."

His heart tore in two. Unable to hold himself back any longer, he engulfed her in his arms and held her close. How had he not known the pain she'd lived with? How had he not seen it? "I'll stand up for you, Jude. That might not mean much now, but I'll stand beside you, in front of you, or even a step behind you. How can I even start to make this right?"

She buried her head in his chest and sobs shook her shoulders. Tears soaked through his T-shirt. "Nothing can change the past," she said, a hiccup interrupting her words. "I'm okay, at least as okay as I can be—murdering stalker aside."

He snorted at her attempt to lighten the mood.

"I made it out, but I didn't think about the mess I left behind. I was a kid then, so I didn't see things clearly. Now... now I know I need to figure out how to help Laura. She might hate me, and she has every right too, but I can't sit back and watch her repeat a cycle of abuse she should never have been exposed to in the first place."

Her conviction constricted his chest. If she wanted to help Laura leave her asshole of a boyfriend, maybe that meant she planned to stay in town after the danger passed. He held her tighter, the idea of having her in Pine Valley opening limitless possibilities for a future he'd thought he'd lost.

No.

Her plans didn't mean a darn thing to him. Jude was his ex, a woman who lived through hell but still had broken his heart. Knowing her story explained a lot about why she'd made the decisions she'd made, but it didn't erase everything she'd put him through. Didn't mean they had any business being together.

Focusing on her dilemma, he chose his words with care. "Laura doesn't have a lot of friends in her life outside of Isaac. He keeps her pretty isolated. She quit school and depends on him for everything. I know people have tried to talk to her— tried to help. But..." he lifted his hands, not sure what else to say.

She swished her mouth from side to side. "I need to think of something."

"I'm sure you will." He kissed the top of her head, liking the way she felt against him way too much. "But our first priority is making sure we keep you safe."

She untangled herself from his arms and shoved a hand through her hair. Her eyes were red and puffy, and a world of worry was evident in every line on her face.

He tugged on a strand. "Have I mentioned I like the blond?"

A small smile touched her lips. "You might have mentioned it."

"Good. Can I get you anything? I'm going to clean up dinner. Or did you want to eat more?"

She wrinkled her nose. "I ate plenty. But I think I saw Mia put a six-pack in the fridge. A beer sounds good after dumping my trauma all over you."

Laughing, he stood and crossed to the fridge. "That's not dumping, darlin'. That's sharing."

"Now it's your turn," she said. "I want to know how your mom's doing. She was always so great. I'd love to see her."

He swallowed hard and hid his face in the cool refrigerator. He might not have trauma from the past to unpack, but his present was anything but pretty. And he wasn't quite ready to expose all the ugliness of his reality.

A soft knock on the door had him straightening with a brown bottle in each hand. He tossed one to Jude before hurrying to the door and peeking through the front window to the porch. Twilight had approached, but he didn't need a light to know who stood on the other side of the door.

Opening it wide, he grinned at Chet and Mia. "What are you two doing here?"

Chet waved a deck of cards in the air then shoved past him. "Got off work early. I'm here to catch up with my friend."

Mia gave Wade a quick squeeze. "What he meant to say was, do you mind if we hang out for a while? He'd love to see Jude."

Wade glanced over his shoulder at Jude. She'd stood and hugged Chet tight, the beautiful smile on her face chasing away the lingering cloud of turmoil. No matter how he wanted to spend the rest of the evening, he'd do anything to keep that smile on Jude's face.

Luckily, spending time with two of his favorite people wouldn't be a hardship at all.

14

W ade wiped the cleared-off table with a damp dishrag one last time before taking a seat and nodding toward Chet. "Go ahead and deal."

"Don't have to tell me twice." Chet sank low in the folding chair they'd brought in from the deck. He tossed the cards around in messy piles.

"What are we playing?" Jude asked. The puffiness had eased from around her eyes, although the redness remained.

The last few days had been so heavy, Wade wanted to lighten the mood as best he could. He shot Jude a wink then huddled his cards in his hands. "Five card draw. What else?"

Jude let out such a long, loose laugh and it warmed his soul. "You've got to be kidding me."

Mia frowned as she picked up her own cards and arranged them in one hand. "What's happening?"

"Got me," Chet said, scratching his bearded chin, but he couldn't quite hide his slow grin.

"These jerks, along with our friend Tucker, used to whoop me in poker when we were younger," Jude said. "I never could catch on, and they'd work together to make sure I always got out first. Ate all my poor little pretzels."

"Pretzels?" Mia asked, clearly puzzled.

As if on cue, Chet plucked an unopened bag of pretzel sticks from beside his chair.

Jude groaned and let her head fall to the table.

Chuckling, Wade opened the bag and handed them each a pile of the fake currency. "We never had any money or poker chips when we played, so we always used pretzels. Jude just wanted to eat them, but we told her she couldn't unless she won—which she never did."

Jude snapped up her head and pointed a finger at Wade then Chet. "You guys cheated."

Wade threw up his palms. "I would never, and I'm appalled you'd accuse me."

She rolled her eyes. "I don't want to hear it."

"Well, I suck at poker," Mia said. "So don't worry, you won't be the last one out this time. I'll be gone way before anyone else. And don't even think about scolding me for eating my currency."

"I think Chet stacked the deck," Jude said, studying her hand. "That was always your favorite trick. Remember the time Laurie caught you cheating? She was so mad. Picked up the whole deck and tossed it across the room." She winced then shot a nervous glance at Mia. "I'm sorry. Maybe I shouldn't..."

"Don't you dare apologize," Chet said, smiling. "We talk about Laurie and Riley a lot. It's nice to tell old stories."

Mia reached for his hand. "I wish I could have met them."

A ping of sadness echoed inside Wade. He was happy as hell Chet had found Mia, but it'd never erase the pain of what had happened to Laurie and Riley. Chet's wife and daughter would always be missed, but it was nice to keep their memories alive. Something Chet never allowed before he'd fallen for Mia.

Jude plucked a pretzel from her pile and hoisted it in the

air. "Well then, to Laurie. And Riley, who I'd give anything to have met." Her voice caught and tears made the blue of her eyes shimmer.

Chet dipped his chin and picked up a pretzel of his own.

Wade and Mia followed suit, saluting the missing members of their circle who'd never be forgotten.

The next two hours were filled with laughs, reminiscing, and Jude asking Mia countless questions. Wrigley and Macey slept by the fire, heads popping up at sudden shouts or rounds of laughter. As Chet and Mia's pretzel piles dwindled, Jude's smile grew. A lot had changed since the last time they'd sat at a table and played a friendly game of cards, but he'd never expected Jude to be good at poker.

"Four of a kind," she said, a smug grin lifted one side of her mouth. She swooped her hand over her bounty and pulled it into her growing pile. "I won again."

Shaking his head, Wade tipped back in his chair. He only had a few pretzels left, and his pride dangled by a string. "How are you doing this? You were always so bad at this game."

She shrugged and shuffled the cards. "Maybe I wasn't as bad as you thought."

"No," Chet said. "You were pretty terrible."

"Or was I a silly girl who didn't want to injure her boyfriend's confidence and also hated playing cards?"

"What?" Chet and Wade shouted in unison.

She giggled. "Laurie hated this dumb game, too. We'd pretend to lose so we could stop playing. When she threw those cards? We wanted to go to a movie you guys wouldn't have taken us to. Gave us the perfect excuse to leave in a huff and go without you two following."

Wade's jaw dropped. "Are you kidding me? All that time, it was just a lie?"

The accusation exploded in the room like a grenade, as though the statement encompassed more than two teenage girls tricking their boyfriends a decade ago. It was like he'd scraped up the balm they'd slapped over the ugly truth of all the circumstances that had led them to this place.

The teasing glint left her eyes, all amusement gone from her smile. "No. Not a lie," she said, her stare fixed squarely on him. "Nothing about what happened back then was a lie."

He swallowed hard, unsure of how to respond. An awkward silence settled over the table, louder than he thought possible. Dammit, he was an idiot to think a friendly game of poker could erase the dark cloud that hovered above him since he'd laid eyes on Jude the night before. Erase the tension and simmering bitterness from the conversation he and Jude hadn't finished before Chet and Mia arrived.

"It's getting late," Mia said, raising to her feet. "Chet and I should get back home. Early mornings tomorrow."

Chet scooped all the cards from the table and shoved them back in their holder.

"I'm sorry," Jude said. "I made it weird. Wade was just teasing, and I turned it into something I shouldn't have."

Standing, Chet covered her hand with his. "I've told you once. Stop apologizing. Speak your truth, no matter how weird it makes shit."

A pinch of admiration squeezed Wade's chest. Chet had come a long way in a very short amount of time, and his words were wiser than anything Wade had said to Jude. And he hoped she listened. That she'd keep talking, keep confiding in him, until there was no more weirdness left in her confessions.

But the question remained. Could he do the same? Could he open up about his life and his mom and what he'd endured in the years since she'd been away? He mentally rolled his eyes as he watched his friends leave.

It didn't matter what he told Jude. She didn't need to know, and there was no reason to strengthen any bond he had left with her. Their situation was temporary, and he couldn't lose anymore of himself to Jude than he already had.

THE ENERGY SHIFTED with the closing door, and Jude jumped to her feet to clean off the remnants of their game. "This was nice. I like Mia. She seems really good for Chet."

"Yeah," Wade said, scratching the back of his neck. "Listen, do you mind if I grab a shower? It's been a long day and I didn't get a chance to take one earlier."

The uneasiness in his tone had her focusing way too hard on the pretzels she shoveled back into the bag. Throwing them away seemed liked a waste, even though there was no way she'd eat any of them after they'd been touched by so many people. "Go for it. I'll clean up."

She busied herself righting the small kitchen until she heard the bathroom door close and the shower turn on. A well of frustration bubbled inside her. She dropped into a hard chair and folded over the table, using her crossed arms to cover the top of her head. She was thirty years old, and her life was a mess.

Even before the nightmare she currently was fighting to survive, things hadn't been easy. Yes, she loved being a photographer. But other than her camera and her passion, she had nothing. She was no more than a drifter, a tumbleweed rolling from town to town with no connections, no plan, no real life.

No matter what, she couldn't go back to such a meaningless existence. Back to a life without friends and laughter and impromptu poker games.

A life without Wade.

The thought straightened her spine and made her heart seize. She and Wade had bounced between falling into an old rhythm, battling through nerve-fraying awkwardness, and her spilling long-held family secrets. She'd never felt closer to him, yet at the same time farther away. Their relationship—their past—was too messy. Riddled with too much pain to even think there was a chance at a future with him.

But the idea of losing Wade again squeezed her chest so tightly she could barely breath.

The creaking of the shifting house reached her ears, and she stilled, paying attention to the noise she swore was at the back of the duplex. A swift flash of jealousy struck her like a bolt of lightning. Probably Chet and Mia sneaking onto the back deck with a warm blanket to snuggle in and a bottle of wine. Longing reverberated inside her. She used to have someone to steal kisses with and cuddle under the stars.

And that man was naked and standing under a warm spray of water twenty feet away.

Heat flamed her cheeks. She should go to bed. The last thing she needed was to be sitting here all hot and bothered with a headful of nostalgia when Wade waltzed out of the bathroom. Besides, she didn't want to hear any other sounds that may or may not leak into the apartment from the doting couple.

Decision made, she stood and walked to the front door to double check the locks then shut off the light for the kitchen and living room. The sun had set, and shadows moved around her. More creaking, along with the distinct silence that told her Wade was out of the shower, set her nerves on edge.

As if sensing her anxiety, Macey stood from her spot beside the fireplace and let out a low growl.

"You're fine, girl. Just a weird night. Let's head to bed." She took a step toward the hall, determined to be behind her closed bedroom door before Wade came out of the bathroom looking scrumptious.

A loud screech, like the sound of furniture dragging across the deck, raised the hairs on her arm. A dark shadow loomed across the living room floor, swallowing the small dog in the corner. Confusion rippled her forehead, and she turned toward the glass sliding door.

Moonlight outlined the frame of a man. Panic filled her as he pointed a gun at her chest.

Bang!

She screamed and dove for the floor. Glass shattered and Macey barked. Fear pounded a frantic beat inside her skull and she stayed on the ground, scrambling toward something to hide behind. She lunged for the couch, pulse racing.

Footsteps crunched on glass. A low laugh twisted her insides. "You really thought I wouldn't find you? I mean, you made it more interesting than I expected. But your time's up."

A cry caught in her throat. She darted around the couch. Tears welled in her eyes. She didn't want to die. Not like this. Being hunted down like a terrified animal.

The footsteps got closer. "No use running. Might as well make this easy on yourself. There's no way out."

A hard yank on her foot dragged her backward. She clawed at the ground, thrashing her body. "Help!" she yelled.

A hard twist on her ankle flipped her to her back. The man stood over her, gun pointed at her head. "No one can help you now."

15

Stepping out of the shower, Wade wrapped a cotton towel around his waist and scrubbed another one over his head. The shower hadn't been as long as he'd wanted—or as cold as he needed—to get Jude out of his system. A weird vibe hovered between them, and he didn't know how to get rid of it.

Or if he should even try.

Best to just keep going through the motions until everything played out, and he could go back to a regular life. A life where Jude was gone, and he was as far away as possible from any woman who might break his heart. He'd had enough heartbreak to handle with his mom. He couldn't let Jude get close just to clobber him over the head when things didn't work out.

Thoroughly dry, he tossed the damp towels over the lip of the tub and hurried into his clothes. Baggy sweatpants and a hoodie to finish off the evening with a casual conversation before retreating to his room for the rest of night. He needed some distance from Jude. Not a cozy winter evening spent in front of a fire while they continued to spill their secrets.

Bang!

His heart jumped into his throat. A gunshot came from inside the house.

Jude!

His pulse raced as he grabbed the door handle and crept out of the room. The cold floors barely registered on his bare feet as adrenaline pumped through his veins. A low voice caught his attention, the sound of scurrying and crunching of glass raising the hair on his arms. Dammit, he should have grabbed his gun.

Please God let Jude be alive. Don't let me be too late.

Forcing his breathing to slow, he moved methodically down the hall. He fisted his hands at his sides, ready to do whatever he needed to protect Jude. He pressed his back against the wall and rounded the corner. Terror tightened his throat.

Jude lay sprawled on her back on the rug in front of the couch. Macey barked in the corner of the room. Benji stood in front of her, a gun aimed at her head.

Ice chilled the blood in Wade's veins. He charged, wrapping his arms around Benji's waist and slamming him to the ground. The jarring impact against his chest stole the air from his lungs. Sweat coated his palms. Fear climbed up his spine as he scrambled for the weapon.

Benji twisted, bucking and shifting his body to turn onto his back. He kept a firm grip on the gun and swung it toward Jude who scurried to her feet.

No way in hell would Wade let this bastard put a bullet in Jude. He pummeled his fist into Benji's face. Blood squirted from his mouth.

Heavy pounding sounded from the front door and mixed with the chaos of the room.

"Get the door," he yelled at Jude as a bit of relief pushed through his fear. Help was here, probably Chet charging to the rescue after hearing the gunshot.

Benji squirmed beneath him.

Wade hit him again, then circled his wrist and slammed it against the ground until the gun came loose.

Benji shot his head forward. His forehead crunched against Wade's nose.

Pain erupted in Wade's skull and stars burst behind his eyes. He fell backward and lost his hold of Benji.

A small sob came from Jude, and she sprinted for the door. She battled with the lock as the pounding continued from the other side.

Benji lurched forward, one arm wrapping around Wade's waist while reaching the other out to battle for the weapon.

Partially pinned to the ground, Wade shifted his weight and planted his fist in Benji's nose. A sickening crunch gave him a brief moment of satisfaction before he stretched as far as he could toward the gun.

Benji reared back, eyes wide as he flicked his glance between Wade, the gun, and the commotion threatening to burst through the door before Jude could even open it. He tightened his jaw, defeat clear in his scowl, and sprang to his feet before sprinting toward the shattered slider at the back of the home.

Wade snatched up the gun, hurried to his feet, and rushed forward. Shards of glass pierced the bottoms of his feet, slowing his pace. But he kept moving, wincing as pain shot up his legs. Cold air skimmed his face and he leapt onto the deck as Benji pounded down the stairs and darted toward the surrounding forest. Wade planted his feet on the rough wooden planks, lifted the gun, and fired. The blast split his eardrums, the backfire vibrating his arm.

Benji ran faster, putting more and more distance between them until he disappeared into the trees.

Chet appeared on the deck. "Dude, you okay? Are you hurt?"

"I'm fine, but he's getting away. We need to go after him." He started for the steps but a heavy hand on his shoulder stopped him.

"You're bleeding." Chet pointed at the ground.

Wade dropped his gaze then lifted his feet. Pieces of glass were wedged in his flesh, blood seeping from a handful of cuts. "It doesn't matter. I'll grab some shoes and have someone look at them later. We have to go after him."

"No, you need to get back inside and take care of Jude. I called the police, and Grace is on her way. She can track him better than either of us. I know it's frustrating to see him slip away, but Jude needs you now."

Reality crashed down on him. He hadn't checked to make sure Jude was okay. He shoved past Chet, ignoring the jabs of pain as fresh punctures pierced his tender skin, and ran back inside. "Jude!"

Jude huddled in the kitchen, her arms hugging her chest tightly and sobs racking her slender body. Her eyes were wide, her skin so damn pale.

He rushed to her and pulled her into his arms, absorbing her tears and her fear. He cradled her head in his palm. "I got ya, now. Everything's going to be all right." He pressed his lips to her ear, hating how she shook against him.

She fisted his shirt and buried her face in his neck. "I was so scared. I thought I was going to die. Then I thought you'd die and I just...oh God. I don't want to be the reason you're hurt. Not now and not ever."

"Shhh, it's okay." He rubbed a hand in a small circle on her back. "I'm fine. You're fine."

As he held her, adrenaline leaked from his system. His heartrate slowed, his breathing evened out, and he tried to erase the image of the man with a gun pointed at Jude. A ball of emotion lodged in his throat. He would have killed Benji tonight if the bastard hadn't run away. If there was a next time, he wouldn't let him get away again.

THE SMALL APARTMENT bustled with activity. Jude pulled a blanket tighter over her shoulders and stayed rooted at Wade's side, watching the organized chaos from the couch. Her body had finally stopped shaking, but the terror had yet to leave her system.

She wasn't sure it ever would.

Benji Blitz hadn't laid a hand on her like last time, but this had been different. Laying helpless on her back with a gun pointed at her head was the scariest thing she'd ever experienced. She'd been convinced her life was over—had wondered what the bullet ripping into her skull would feel like or if she'd leave anyone behind who'd even miss her. And worst yet, a million thoughts had flashed through her mind about all the mistakes she'd made and how she'd never be able to fix them.

An emergency responder kneeled in front of Wade and finished wrapping a bandage around his foot. "All right. You're cleaned up and good to go. Take over-the-counter pain pills and try to stay off your feet. You'll be a little tender for a few days."

"Thanks, Al. Appreciate it."

Al stood and stared down at Jude, his lips pressed in a thin line. The bright lights illuminating the room beat down on him and showcased his dark hair and babyface. "You need rest, too. You might not have been physically injured, but tonight was traumatic as hell. Don't take that lightly."

"I won't," she said. Jude planned on finding a bed, hiding under a blanket, and not getting up for a week.

"Y'all have a good night." Al dipped his chin, gathered his first aid kit, and headed toward the door.

"Here, honey," Mia said, skirting the corner of the sofa. "Have some tea. I don't know why, but something hot always seems to help."

Jude couldn't even manage a small smile when she accepted the mug and cradled it in her hands.

"Wade, would you like anything?" Mia asked.

"Something a lot stronger than that tea," he said, snorting as he kept one arm tucked firmly around her shoulders.

"Let's wait for the police to finish up then we'll see what we got." She winked then settled in the armchair, Wrigley glued himself to her side as Macey jumped into her lap.

Jude glanced over her shoulder at the two officers—Cruz and his twin brother Lincoln—talking to a woman and Chet on the deck. "What are they talking about? And who's out there with them?"

As if Cruz had heard her question, the foursome marched through the space where a sliding door should've been. Mia had cleaned up the shattered glass after the police had shown up, insisting Jude relax and focus on giving her statement to Cruz.

Chet stepped up behind Mia and placed a hand on her shoulder. "How you two holding up?"

Jude shrugged and snuggled closer to Wade's side. She kept glancing at the busted door, waiting for Benji to come storming back inside to kill her. Logic told her that wouldn't happen. He'd been injured and no way he'd come back with the lights blazing and place packed, but she couldn't help the tremors shaking her insides. "Did you find him?"

Cruz, Lincoln and the mystery woman stood in front of the fireplace in a line—all with grim faces that answered her question before anyone spoke.

The woman shook her head, causing her long dark braid to sway behind her. "No, but I followed his tracks into the woods. There was some blood—Wade, you must have clocked the bastard good—and it looks like he found an old dirt lane to park his car. He'd taken off before we got to him." She aimed her irritated gaze toward Jude, a slight smile softening her hard edges. "I'm Grace, by the way. Nice to meet you, although sorry this is how."

Jude offered a small wave. "How did he know I was here?"

"My guess is he spotted you at the hospital and followed you. Scoped out the place and formed a plan to hide the car and come up to the house at nightfall," Cruz said.

"Could you follow the tire marks Grace found?" Wade asked.

"We did," Lincoln said. "But they led to the highway. Not much we could do from there. We're assuming he's driving the same car you spotted leaving your restaurant earlier. We ran those plates, by the way, and the vehicle was reported stolen in Elm Ridge. Presumably after his altercation with Jude's brother."

A fresh wave of tears stung her eyes. She still hadn't heard from Brandon, which meant Matthew hadn't woken. But she couldn't think about that right now. Not with everything else going on. "So what do I do?"

Lincoln rubbed a palm over his scruffy beard then approached her and crouched so they were eye to eye. "You don't know me. Don't know us." He swiped a hand behind him. "But everyone here wants to keep you safe. I spoke with my wife, Brooke, who runs the retreat Cruz told you about before. I understand your trepidation, but I really believe it's the best option right now. The best place to keep you safe. Most of the staff are trained former officers, and I live on site as well. You can trust us. I promise you."

The earnestness in his blue eyes combined with her need to believe that something could protect her and weakened her resolve. That plus the fact she didn't have any other options. "How do I know he won't follow me there, too? He could be waiting to see where I go so he can show up again."

"I won't lie, that's a possibility. But you can't stay here. You can't go back to Wade's. Where else can you stay?"

Grace took a step forward. "I get the whole *don't trust those who haven't earned it* thing. But Crossroads Mountain Retreat isn't just full of random people trying to get their lives back on track. We're family. And now, you're one of us."

The conviction in her tone furrowed Jude's brow. "One of you? How do you figure?"

Grace shrugged. "I don't know your story, but you're important to Wade. You're important to Chet and Mia. That means you're important to the rest of us. We've got you."

"What do you say?" Wade asked. "Willing to give it a try?"

She bit her thumbnail, considering everything that had been thrown at her. But there was really only one choice, all other options ripped away. "Fine. I'll go to Crossroads Mountain Retreat."

16

Cold night air swirled around Jude as she jumped out of Officer Lincoln Sawyer's truck and stood in front of the lodge at Crossroads Mountain Retreat. After leaving Chet's place, she and Wade were shuttled to the retreat. Everyone had agreed it was safest for them to ride with Lincoln since his normal routine brought him back there anyway. Mia and Chet would drop off Wade's truck in the morning.

She stood beside Wade, mouth open and eyes wide. A three-story log cabin styled building sprawled out in front of her. An inviting porch wrapped around to the back, twinkle lights strung along the railing and a smattering of wooden rocking chairs provided plenty of seating for relaxing and enjoying the view of the mountains on the horizon. "This is not what I expected."

Lincoln climbed out of the driver's side and came up beside her. "What'd you think you'd find? A bunch of tents set up in the woods?"

Wade chuckled. "More like some spider infested cabins with creaky bunk beds and holes in the roof."

"Excuse me?" Lincoln asked, frowning.

The day had been long as hell, but Jude couldn't help smiling at the picture Wade painted and how completely different it was from what was in front of her. The sound of the surrounding nature wasn't as loud as the nights she'd spent here years before when the weather was warmer, but it still carried a hundred memories. "Wade and I used to come here in the summer when we were kids. Back when it was still a camp."

"Really? Wade never mentioned that," Lincoln said.

Wade shrugged and shifted the bags he carried to his shoulder.

"Well, my wife would love to hear stories if and when you're up for it."

The giant double doors opened, and a petite woman with long brown hair stepped outside and lifted her arm above her head in an enthusiastic wave. A tan dog stood beside her. "Hey there! Come on in."

Jude waited for Lincoln to take the lead then walked beside Wade as they crossed the parking lot and climbed the porch steps.

Macey pranced around the other dog, tail wagging.

Nerves danced in the pit of Jude's stomach, and she tightened her grip on the straps of her backpack. She wanted to believe she'd be safe here, that she could trust the community of people who'd come together to help her. But it was damn hard to let her guard down and believe this tiny woman could do anything to protect her.

The woman extended a hand and offered a sweet smile. "Hi. I'm Brooke, and this this Wyatt." She dipped her chin toward the dog. "I'm so sorry for your troubles but glad to meet you."

Jude accepted her hand and returned the smile. "Thanks for having me. I really appreciate it. I know the circumstances are...unique."

"Trust me. We've experienced more than our fair share of unique experiences here in the last few years. We've got you."

Brooke gave Lincoln a small kiss on the cheek then opened the door, waiting for the group to step inside before entering behind them.

Astonishment slowed Jude's steps. She swept her gaze up to the high ceilings, loving the dark beams that zigzagged above her. A large stone hearth climbed a nearby wall, stretching all three stories, with a fire blazing inside the deep pit. Burgundy rugs dotted the mahogany floors, anchoring multiple seating areas with deep brown furniture and glossy stands. Floor-to-ceiling windows took up the far wall, no doubt providing a magnificent view during the day.

"Most guests stay in the cabins behind the lodge, but I figured you'd feel safer in here. The place is locked up tight, we have cameras along the outside of the building, and there's always at least one staff member here at all times. Tonight, that will be me."

"What? No, that's not necessary. I'm already putting you out enough."

Brooke waved a hand through the air as if batting away her argument. "Nonsense. Lincoln and I have a big night planned of organizing files and cleaning gym equipment. What every newlywed looks forward to, right?"

Lincoln winced then wrapped an arm around his wife's waist. "I'm at your disposal."

The simple gesture and easy acceptance squeezed Jude's chest. She'd just met Brooke and Lincoln, but their connection was easy to see, their love pure. She'd had that once with Wade. They'd been so young, but she'd always wondered if those untested and natural feelings would have continued to develop or fizzle out with the pressures of adulthood.

She chanced a peek at Wade, whose attention was fixed squarely on her. Heat climbed the back of her neck, but she didn't break their connection. Didn't look away from the longing and worry and hint of pain in his eyes.

No, despite years and miles apart, nothing had fizzled between her and Wade. But she had no idea what that meant for a future, and she didn't have the energy to try and figure it out right now.

"Cruz made it sound like you wanted to bunk together, so I put you in the second room to the left. Wade, you know where it is. You two can head down, or I can show Jude around if she wants."

Jude swallowed hard, finally tearing her gaze from Wade. "A tour isn't necessary. I'm pretty exhausted."

"I understand. Maybe tomorrow, if you're up for it. Make yourself at home while you're here. Wade knows his way around but make him give you my phone number. Call any time, okay?" Brooke handed her a key.

Jude nodded. "Okay. Thank you."

"Goodnight, guys. Thanks again and let us know if you find Benji." Wade captured her hand and led her down a wide corridor, stopping in front of the door Brooke had mentioned. "Here we are."

She used the key, heard the lock click, then pushed open the door.

Macey bolted inside, jumped on the couch, and curled into a ball.

The room was just as cute as the rest of the lodge she'd seen. An open concept with a miniature version of the fireplace on the far wall, a loveseat and couch facing it, along with a rocking chair in the corner. A two-person table sat on the tiled kitchen floor, and a queen-sized bed took up the far corner.

The door closed behind her. She jumped then swiveled around.

Wade dropped his bags to the floor and grimaced. "Sorry."

She pressed a hand to her heart, willing it to slow down. "For what? Closing the door? Geez, I'm wound so freaking tight.

I just want this day to be over—I want this nightmare to be over."

The numbness that had encased her since escaping the clutches of the man who wanted to kill her slowly melted away. She wanted it back, wanted it to surround her and paralyze all her emotions so she didn't have to be so damn scared. Tears pressed against the backs of her eyes, her breaths hiking high in her throat yet refusing to leave her mouth.

"Hey, now," Wade said, hurrying to her and gathering her in his arms. "You have an entire village looking after you."

She sniffed back more useless tears. "I don't want to think about it anymore. I just want to go to sleep and forget everything for a few hours, but every time I close my eyes all I see is his face and the gun. I hear his voice. I relive you running out of that apartment and the fear I felt when I didn't know if you'd come back."

He held her closer and pressed his lips to the side of her face. "I did come back, and I'm fine. We're both going to be fine."

His words broke something loose inside her, his arms comforted her in a way she hadn't had for years. She melted against him, never wanting him to let her go.

The thought struck her like a clap of thunder, and she pulled away. She was getting too comfortable. Relying too heavily on the one person she should be staying away from.

Wade frowned and ripples stretched the length of his forehead. "What's wrong? What do you need?"

She considered the question and only one answer dominated her mind. And for this one night, it's the only answer she wanted. "You, Wade. I need you."

~

JUDE'S WHISPERED words stole Wade's breath and made his knees a little wobbly. He tightened his grip around her slim waist. He'd spent years wishing for Jude to come back into his life, to return to Pine Valley and tell him she'd been wrong and still loved him. Still wanted a future with him.

But as much as he wanted to be exactly what Jude needed in this moment, he wasn't sure if swooping in with no conversation about what it meant was the smartest idea.

Unwrapping one arm from around her, he cradled her cheek with his palm. He had to tread lightly. His feelings about Jude were muddled, and he didn't want to ruin anything by not picking his words right. "What do you mean by you need me? Darlin' I'm right here."

She stared up at him with wide, blue eyes, her jaw set in the determined way he'd seen way too many times. "Are you going to make me spell it out for you?"

He grinned, loving the sass sparking in her voice. He'd seen glimmers of the spitfire he'd known and loved, but she'd been hidden behind a wall of fear for the most part. "Maybe. I don't want to misconstrue what you mean. I'm just a dumb bar owner."

"You've never been a dumb anything. But in case there's any misunderstanding..." She lifted up on her toes and pressed her mouth to his.

Stars exploded behind his eyelids. The soft pillow of her lips molded to his, as familiar as his own two hands. Her taste was the same with a hint of something different—something foreign and intoxicating. He moved against her, deepening the kiss, holding her close. His heart fluttered in his chest as though it'd take flight.

With labored breath, he gripped her hips and forced his mouth from hers. "Are you sure you want this? You want me?"

Her lips were red and swollen, and her hair spilled around her face. She braced her hands on his and squeezed. "I've never been so sure of anything in my life. For tonight, I just want to forget about all my troubles. I just want to feel loved."

Her words jolted him like an electric shock and tore him in two. One part of him wanted to spend the night forgetting their troubles. The other cared too much to chance what they could have by falling into bed and doing something she might regret in the morning.

"Wade?" She lifted a palm and rested it on his jawline. "Please."

Her simple request undid him and sent all logic crashing to his feet. He couldn't refuse her even if he wanted to. And Lord help him...he didn't want to.

With no more words, no more arguments, no more resistance he lifted her into his arms and carried her to the bed. He didn't know what tomorrow or the next day would bring, but right now, he didn't care. If he only had one more night with Jude, he'd make sure it was the best damn nights of their lives.

17

The distant ring of a phone penetrated the thick fog keeping Wade in a peaceful slumber. He ignored the invasion, instead wrapping his arms tighter around Jude and fitting her perfectly against the curve of his body.

Her low hum and the wriggling of her ass told him he'd made the right decision.

He pressed his lips to the tender spot behind her ear. Morning sun might be streaming in through the window, but they didn't have anywhere to be. Who said they couldn't extend their delicious night into the next? He planned to only leave the bed to grab some food and rehydrate. He inched his hand lower on Jude's stomach. The warmth of her body and squirming of her hips urged him on.

The ringing stopped for a brief second before starting up again.

Jude giggled. "You might want to see who's calling. It could be important."

He groaned, her words sobering him. Too much was happening for him to shut off the world. Especially when someone was trying repeatedly to get ahold of him. "Do I have to?"

"I'll make it easy for you." Shifting to face him, she pressed a kiss to his lips then reached over him to scoop up his phone. Her body stiffened for a beat before thrusting his device at him. "Here."

He bit back a grimace at the name on the screen then shimmied to sit up and throw his legs over the side of the bed. Summer could be forward, but she only called when it had to do with his mama. "Hey," he said, finally answering the call.

"Hi, Wade. Hope I didn't wake you, but I worked the night shift, and your mom was pretty agitated. Hard to get to sleep and fought me about taking her medicine. She mentioned you didn't come in to see her yesterday. You know how she gets when her routine is disrupted."

He hung his head, guilt burrowing into his chest. Yesterday had been so hectic, he hadn't checked in on his mom like he always did on Sundays. Even if he couldn't visit, he'd at least call.

A shift in the bed had him glancing over his shoulder. Jude sat with her feet tucked under her and back pressed against the headboard. She kept her gaze on the colorful quilt. "Give me a second, okay?" he whispered to Jude, his hand over the speaker on his phone so Summer couldn't hear.

Jude pressed her mouth in a firm line and nodded.

He pushed to his feet and hurried to the bathroom, closing the door so Jude couldn't overhear his conversation. He hadn't told her about his mother's condition, and he didn't want her to find out about it like this.

"Wade? You still there?"

"Yeah, sorry." He sat on the edge of the tub and pinched the bridge of his nose. "How was my mama when you left this morning?"

"Still sleeping."

"That's not good. She'll be off all day."

"That's why I'm calling," Summer continued. "I know the restaurant is closed on Mondays. If you can get to the nursing home and visit with her soon, it might help put her on a better path for the rest of the day."

He squeezed his eyes shut and willed a solution to come to mind. No way he could leave Jude to go see his mom. Not only would it make her more vulnerable—even within the safe walls of the retreat—but Benji could spot him and follow him back to Jude. "I'll call her."

A beat of silence pulsed on the phone. "Are you sure you can't make the time for her today?"

The question was like a knife in the gut. His entire life revolved around making sure his mom had everything she needed. Being the reason she'd be unsettled and more confused than normal hurt his heart, but he didn't see an alternative. "I'll try, but some things are happening that don't make it easy."

"What things?"

"Things I can't talk about. Listen, I appreciate the heads up about Mama and the fact you're looking out for her. But I've got to go."

"Okay, but I don't want to only look out for your mama. I'm here for you, too."

Tension built in his head. He hated when Summer tried to make more of their relationship than was there. He didn't want to be a dick, but he also didn't want to lead her on. "You're a good friend. Talk later."

Disconnecting, he stood and blew out a long breath before dialing his mom. The line rang until voicemail picked up. He left a quick message, ended the call, and left the bathroom. His morning plans had been interrupted, but maybe he could pick up where he'd left off. Warm, snuggled in bed, and ready to take things to the next level.

But the bed was empty, the sheets a rumpled mess and the covers on the floor. "Jude?"

The banging of a cabinet door made him wince.

Macey's head whipped up from her spot on the couch.

"Is there food in here?" Jude asked, her voice clipped and tight. "I'm starving and all I can find is instant coffee and boxed macaroni and cheese."

Wade snorted out a laugh.

Jude whirled around to face him, a tin of coffee in her hand. Her blond hair was a tousled mess and the bruise around her eye had faded. But it was her deep frown that made his stomach muscles clench. "What's so funny?"

"Sorry," he said. "Brooke probably didn't have a chance to stock the kitchen for us since our visit was last-minute, but it's a well-known secret she doesn't usually put much in the rooms. She wants the guests to mingle, not shut themselves off in their own rooms. Hunger's a good motivator to get them up to the lodge."

She gave him her back and tossed the tin on the counter. "That's not the only motivator to get out of this room," she said, half under her breath.

"Excuse me?" He couldn't have heard her right. Minutes before she'd been wrapped around him in the cotton sheets. Now venom shook her words. Tension made her body straight and rigid as a board.

"Nothing. Just hungry." She spun around to face him again. "Where do we go for breakfast?"

He wanted to close the space between them. Erase the unease and twinge of fear from her eyes. But his feet stayed planted, his mind in overdrive as he fumbled with his thoughts. "Breakfast's served in the dining room, or we can head to the kitchen. Chet will be in there cookin' and will make whatever you want."

"Okay. I'll throw on some clothes and run a brush through my hair." Dropping her chin, she tried to move past him.

He caught hold of her wrist, halting her progress. Forcing her to look at him. "Are you all right?"

"I'm fine."

He let her pass, hating the weird energy back between them. He didn't know much about women, but he knew one thing. When she said she was fine, she was anything but.

THE SMELL of salty goodness and a desperate need for some space from Wade quickened Jude's pace toward the kitchen. Breakfast wouldn't be served in the dining room for another thirty minutes, and she didn't have any desire to be in a room full of strangers anyway. She'd much prefer to grab some food from Chet then find a space to sit and shovel through the avalanche of emotions weighing her down.

She'd been hasty last night. Falling into bed with Wade had seemed like the best and easiest decision she could ever make at the time. But seeing another woman's name on his phone so early in the morning—followed by his secretive nature when he answered—told her she'd acted foolishly. Was it the blond from the bar? The one who'd shown up at Chet's? Jealousy scalded her veins, and she fisted her hands at her sides.

It didn't matter. Wade wasn't her boyfriend. He was a grown ass man who could do what he wanted, when he wanted, with whoever he wanted. And it was her own stupid pride that caused this boulder in the pit of her stomach. Nothing more.

Wade touched the small of her back and gestured toward a wide doorway.

She hurried ahead, avoiding his touch and following her nose into the kitchen. Black and white tile covered the floor. Dark mahogany cabinets lined the walls, interrupted by industrial grade stainless steel appliances, and wooden beams criss-crossed the ceiling, making square indents. A large island dominated the center of the room, filled with platters of pastries and bowls of breakfast meats.

"Mornin'," Chet said, turning to offer a quick smile before pulling a tray of something from the oven.

Wade sniffed then groaned. "You made cinnamon rolls?"

A tall, willowy woman with long auburn hair in a low pony-tail wiped her hands on the apron tied around her slim waist. "You're not the only one surprised he's making them on a Monday. Chet's a creature of habit, and you must be the reason that habit was changed. I'm Zoe, Cruz's girlfriend." She hurried to Jude and pulled her in for a quick hug. "So nice to meet you."

A few days ago, being hugged by a stranger would have raised Jude's hackles, but she couldn't resist the sincerity dripping from everyone she'd met since being back in town. "I'm Jude. Nice to meet you, too."

"Has Cruz called you this morning?" she asked, crossing to the giant refrigerator and pulling out bowls filled with diced fruit.

"No, why?" Wade asked. "Did something happen?"

Zoe shook her head. "Nah. That detective from Mill Harbor got into town early this morning. Wasn't sure if he reached out yet. I'm sure he will soon."

A shiver raced down Jude's spine. She'd made up her mind to speak with anyone who could help but the idea of bringing in someone else from the town she'd run from didn't sit well with her.

"Y'all can worry about that later," Chet said. "Grab some food first. Can I whip something up for you?"

"I know what they want." Zoe winked then swiveled around to scoop cinnamon rolls from a pan on the marble counter. She handed one plate to Jude, one to Wade. "Coffee?"

"As long as it's not instant," Jude said, wrinkling her nose.

Zoe chuckled and poured two mugs. "You guys eating in here or want me to take these into the dining room?"

"Here's fine." Jude set her plate on the island and settled onto a stool. She peeled off a flaky chunk of pastry and slid into her mouth. "Holy crap, Chet. You made this?"

"Don't act so surprised." He turned back to the stove and stirred whatever was in the pan.

She accepted the warm mug from Zoe and took a sip. "Only thing I've ever seen you make is a bowl of cereal."

Chet shot her a scowl, a small grin poking through his beard, then went back to his cooking.

The slapping of hurried footsteps approached the kitchen, and Jude stiffened.

A woman with long blond hair poked her head inside. "Zoe, we need to head into the studio."

"Tasha?" Wade asked, mouth agape. "Your hair."

A light blush swept over her pale cheeks. "You like it? I just dyed it yesterday."

"Looks great," Wade said. "I wouldn't have even recognized you."

Jealously swept through Jude, and she worked her jaw back and forth. How many beautiful blonds roamed around Wade, batting their eyelashes and blushing at his dimples?

Zoe untied her apron and hung it on a hook by the door. "I told her I feel like I have a new employee to train. The blond is so different than the dark hair. I love it, though."

"Everyone's changing their hair color around here," Wade said, shooting Jude a wink.

She managed a small smile, touching her own locks. She'd dyed hers back to her natural color after the pink didn't work to keep her safe. The petite woman in the doorway with the small mole above her lip was probably just looking for a fun way to pass the time and experiment with her appearance.

Tasha gave her a tentative grin, her gaze landing at her feet.

"Hopefully most people don't comment. I hate being the center of attention. Much better to sit behind a desk at the yoga studio and follow Zoe wherever she needs me. I'm Tasha, by the way."

Jude let her smile grow. "Jude. Nice to meet you." Tasha couldn't be much older than mid-twenties—if that—and the shy way she stayed a little bit hidden behind the doorframe reminded Jude of how she used to put whatever she could between herself and her father. A tingling sensation in the pit of her stomach told her there was more to Tasha than met the eye.

"I know you have a lot going on," Zoe said as she crossed the room toward the door. "But if you get a chance, I teach a yoga class here this evening. I'd love to see you and Wade there."

Wade snorted. "You haven't gotten me in one of those classes yet. Don't think I'll break that streak tonight."

"You never know," Zoe said with a shrug. "Sometimes all we need is the right person to give us a little push...or in your case a shove." With a wave, she disappeared alongside Tasha.

Jude considered her words before focusing questioning eyes on Wade. "A shove, huh? What's that mean?"

Chet let out a low, rumbling laugh.

"Dude, watch it," Wade muttered.

Interesting. She'd been so caught up navigating her past and present dilemma, she hadn't considered who Wade really was now. And Lord knew he hadn't offered much information. If anything, he'd been tight lipped and secretive. She cringed inwardly. Sleeping with him last night might have erased her worries for a few hours, but it had brought nothing but more questions and insecurities with the light of day.

Wade's phone rang, and he fished his device from his pocket before checking the screen.

"Gonna take this call in the bathroom again?" She couldn't help but add a bite of sarcasm to her tone.

Chet pivoted with raised brows.

Color crept up Wade's neck, and he coughed to clear his throat. "Nah. It's Cruz. Probably calling about that detective. You up to speaking with her this morning?"

She nodded. "Might as well get it over with. Not like I have anything better to do." After she got the dreaded meeting out of the way, maybe she could find something to keep herself busy and away from Wade. Last night had been wonderful, but this morning had been a healthy dose of reality.

And this new reality had proven her first instinct correct. She had to keep up her guard around Wade McKenzie.

18

The sweet roll and acidic coffee gurgled in Jude's stomach. She knotted her hands in her lap, staring through the large windows across the gleaming table in the conference room. Cruz had suggested privacy for their meeting with Detective Hocking, and as much as she agreed, the lack of distractions kept her tapping her foot against the floor.

At least the view was spectacular as she waited. Blankets of snow glazed the tops of the mountain peaks. The lake stretched out behind the lodge, and the cabins she spotted tucked into the surrounding forest looked nothing like the bunks she'd stayed in as a kid.

"This place has changed a lot, hasn't it?" Wade leaned back in the chair beside her, gaze fixed outside.

"It really has. Brooke's done an amazing job transforming the campground into a rehabilitation center. I'd love to see more of it. Maybe even check out that yoga class Zoe mentioned later."

"Zoe's always recruiting people. She's been trying to get me into a class for years now. Just not my thing."

She swiveled her chair and studied him. "And what is your thing? Besides blonds." The moment the words were out of her mouth she wished she could take them back.

His face crumbled in confusion. "Excuse me?"

Dammit. Those rounded eyes and crinkled forehead showcased the jolt of pain she'd just caused, but she couldn't stop herself. Not after she'd been so vulnerable with him. First by exposing the ugliness of her past, then by spending the night in his arms. Her heart had been so full while she'd laid in his bed. A feeling of contentment and joy and a rightness she hadn't experienced since she'd left his side so many years ago had left her body humming.

Then he'd jumped out of that same bed they'd shared as soon as another woman called. Escaping into the next room so she couldn't overhear their conversation.

She shot to her feet and moved to stand in front of the windows. "Nothing. Forget it."

The sound of Wade's squeaky chair and tentative footsteps steeled her spine. "I won't forget it. What did you mean?"

With fire flowing through her veins, she crossed her arms and faced him. "Well there's the lady from the bar—the same woman who showed up at Chet's and you were wrapped all around—me, and the perky yoga instructor. I'd ask if there were more I should know about it, but it's not really any of my business. There's nothing between us besides one old friend helping out another."

He winced and scrubbed a hand over his face. "That's all I am to you? An old friend? And what about last night...it didn't mean anything?"

She tightened her jaw, refusing to let a flicker of emotion shine through. "Meant the same to me as it did to you. Which was obvious as soon as you scurried out of bed to talk to another woman."

"That woman called about my mother. And Tasha is a

friend I've probably only said a dozen words to since she moved to town. But if I'm just some guy who doesn't mean anything to you, none of that should matter anyway so what are you all bent out of shape for?"

The venom in his voice stole her anger. She struggled to come up with something more to say, somewhere else to take the conversation, but a knock on the open door sounded before Cruz strolled in with a medium-sized woman with straight black hair and perfectly pressed pant suit.

"Hey, you two," Cruz said, scooting out the chair at the end of the table and setting down a stack of files. "How'd you sleep last night?"

Heat shot through Jude's core. She dropped her face and hurried to her chair, managing to mutter something she hoped sounded like fine.

"Brooke put us up in the lodge," Wade said, not missing a beat and returning to a chair across the wide table.

"Makes sense. Safer than by the lake." Cruz dipped his chin at the woman beside him. "Let me introduce you to Detective Hocking."

Detective Hocking took a step forward and offered a palm to Jude. "Nice to meet you both. Thanks for agreeing to speak with me."

Jude shook her hand. "Whatever I need to do to put this guy behind bars."

Detective Hocking sat beside her then nodded hello to Wade. "I appreciate that. This crime family has infiltrated Mill Harbor and we've been working hard to get them out. If we can connect the boss' nephew to a murder, it might be just what we need to take them down."

Jude swallowed hard. Her situation was scary enough when it started, but finding out how dangerous the people were who were after her made it even more terrifying—and seemingly impossible that she'd be the one who could stop such a powerful family. "Just tell me what you need to know."

For the next thirty minutes, Detective Hocking shuffled through papers, photos and questions until Jude had unloaded every detail she could recall. Jude's throat was dry, and her nerves stretched tighter with each passing second.

Wade stayed quiet, soaking in everything, then picked up a glossy photo. "So this is the nephew? The guy who killed the man in Mill Harbor?"

Detective Hocking nodded. "One and the same. Jude's statement puts him at the crime scene. Her photos are evidence. I have officers searching for him now so we can bring him into the station."

"What do you mean searching for him?" Jude asked, frowning.

"He's been undetectable since all this went down. But I'm positive we'll find him soon. We know all his usual haunts. It won't be long before we catch him."

"And what about Benji Blitz?" Wade asked.

"We haven't found him yet," Cruz cut in. "We have all patrol officers—local and state—on the lookout for him and the car he was in."

Jude squirmed in the leather chair, and its wheels creaked with the motion. She glanced up and caught Wade's eye, and even though their relationship was a bit strained at the moment, it was clear their minds were in the same spot. No matter where she was or how much information she gave the police, she wouldn't be safe until Benji was found.

Detective Hocking rearranged her papers and replaced them in the manila file. "I plan to stay in town for a few more hours then head back home. There's not much more I can do down here. If you need me, don't hesitate to call. But until this is all over, I'd stay put. Sounds like you've landed in the best place to keep you safe with the best people for the job."

Cruz's phone rang, and he pulled it from his pocket. "This is Lincoln. I need to take it."

Jude drummed her thumb along the table, lost in thought. She'd hoped the butterflies constantly swarming in her stomach would dissipate after speaking with the detective, but they'd only multiplied. Maybe she could take that tour of the retreat Brooke had offered and find something to keep her busy.

Wade stroked his fingers through the scruff along his jawline.

A flash of a memory crashed into her mind. Wade's long, strong fingers taking her to heights of pleasure she'd never known, his soft lips and whispered words causing flames to erupt inside her. Last night had certainly erased her problems for a little while. Maybe...

No. Only more problems and a strain on their tenuous relationship came from last night's activities. She'd have to figure out something else.

"Okay. Thanks for letting me know. Detective Hocking and I will meet you at the scene." Cruz's agitated voice snapped her back to the moment.

"What's wrong? What scene?" Jude asked, bouncing her attention between Cruz and Detective Hocking.

Sighing Cruz squeezed the back of his neck. "Well, Benji Blitz was found. He's dead."

"This must be what limbo feels like," Wade said, staring at the door after Cruz and the detective left. He struggled to absorb the bomb that had been thrown.

Jude's skin had paled impossibly further, her blue eyes wide and filled with alarm. "Does that mean this is over?"

Wade shrugged, wishing he had an answer. "Cruz said he'd

call us when he had more details. Benji's car crash was probably an accident with all the injuries from last night. With him out of the picture, and once the nephew up north gets arrested, you'll be in the clear."

Sadness swept through him, followed quickly by guilt. Jude being safe was the only thing that mattered. This slap of despair was the last thing he should be feeling. Jude wasn't his anymore, she wasn't slipping through his fingers, she would just move on to the next phase of her life. With or without him.

Hell, she'd been gone for twelve years. So why did the idea of spending one day without her threaten to bring him to his knees?

Because he still loved her.

Swallowing past the realization, he made a decision. Now that the danger in Jude's present was clearing up, he wanted to focus on her future—and the role he longed to play.

Jude blew out a shaky breath and rubbed her palms up and down the thighs of her jeans. "Every day I think there's no way I'll be more nervous than I was the day before. And every day I find out that's not true. I swear I'm going to jump out of my skin."

He hopped to his feet and wiggled his fingers in a come-here motion. "Let's go."

The V between her eyebrows deepened. "Where?"

"I want you to trust me right now. Can you do that?" He tried to keep the lines of his face passive so she couldn't see how worried he was to hear her answer.

She bit her bottom lip, the hesitation in her eyes sharper than a knife.

"Please."

"Okay," she said, slowly raising to her feet.

He wanted to take her hand, but instead shot off a text to make sure his plan would work. A quick approval was sent back, and he tipped his head toward the door, shoved his hands in his pockets, and led the way out. "We'll need our coats, so we'll stop by the room and grab Macey."

She narrowed her eyes, chin tilted at an angle. "Outside? It's freezing."

"Like I said. Trust me."

He stayed beside her as they walked down the stairs and down the hall to the room they'd shared. He tried his darndest to ignore the bed and piles of rumpled sheets, but he couldn't stop the ache in his chest from spreading through the rest of his body. He'd screwed things up by taking that call into the bathroom. If he wanted any kind of future with Jude, time had come to share every part of himself with her.

Jude shrugged into her leather jacket and snapped on Macey's leash before handing it to him. "All right. Let's head out."

He waited until they stepped into the cold air, the sun bright in the blue sky. "As we walk, I'd like to clear up a few things."

Jude kept her focus fixed on the worn path they walked that wound around to the back of the lodge toward the lake. "We don't have to do this."

"Yes, I do. I didn't handle things well this morning, and I regret that more than you know." He tightened his grip on the leash and wished he had a pair of gloves.

She snorted, the gravel crunching under her shoes combining with the calls of nature from the nearby trees. "What? You wish you'd let the call go to voicemail?"

He grabbed hold of her wrist and turned her toward him. Tiny waves lapped along the lake behind her. "I'll answer Summer's phone calls any time they come."

A wounded expression pinched Jude's face. "Good to know."

"No, you don't understand. Summer works at the nursing home where my mom lives. She's a friend and keeps an eye out, letting me know if Mama's having a hard day or something's agitated her."

Jude's mouth formed a small O but no sound came out.

"Mama had a rough time last night, which means she'll probably have a rough day. I make time to see her on certain days. We keep a pretty rigid schedule to make sure things are consistent as possible for her. It makes her life a little easier. I usually visit on Sundays, and when I didn't show or call, it threw Mama all out of whack." His voice caught on the last word. He hated that his mother lived in such a state that something so small could ruin an entire day.

Jude twisted her hand so it released his grip on her wrist then nestled her palm against his and squeezed. "You never mentioned your mom was in a nursing home. Only that she moved and couldn't take Macey with her."

He shrugged. "It's not easy to talk about with anyone, but especially with you. You knew her so damn well. You have memories of a fun, smart, and vibrant woman. Having to explain her mind is failing her—that I had to sell everything I could in order to afford to put her in a care facility because I couldn't take care of her anymore—isn't something I even know how to do."

"Dementia?" she asked, face falling.

He nodded.

"Oh Wade, I'm so sorry."

The words he was supposed to say sat on the tip of his tongue. It's okay. We're fine. Thanks, but it's not your fault.

But he couldn't make himself spit them out. Because it wasn't okay and no one was fine.

Pressure built behind his eyes, and he sniffed back all the sadness and frustration and fear he constantly carried around with him. "It really, really sucks." For the first time, he said exactly what he wanted, what he felt about watching his mother slip further and further away from him every day.

"I wish I had some magic words to make you feel better," Jude said, voice low and soft. "But I know you're making all the right decisions. Doing everything you can for her."

Her confidence in him misted his eyes. "I doubt myself all the time. I hate that she's not with me. That I'm not the one caring for her. But I just can't. Every spare minute I have, which isn't much, is devoted to her. To being around for whatever she needs. She's the only other blond in my life worth a damn, and the one that means more to me than anything."

She wrinkled her nose. "I'm sorry I said that. I was jealous and spit out something stupid. I wanted to wake up this morning and feel loved, not brushed aside. I never once stopped to consider that your actions had nothing to do with me."

He took a step forward, crowding into her personal space. He didn't want there to be miscommunication, no misunderstanding. "I'm so used to only thinking about me and Mama, and I hate how the way I handled my call with Summer made you feel anything other than adored. Because I adore you, Jude Metcalf. Always have. Always will."

A light blush stained her cheeks and she grinned. "Is that because I'm adorable?"

A hoot of laughter shot from his chest. "You're something all right. And last night was amazing. For so many reasons. But mostly, because holding you in my arms just makes sense. Feels right. Puts all the craziness in our path on another planet. I don't want to give that up."

Her eyes widened. "Maybe that's something we need to think about, once this weird limbo place we've landed is over."

"Okay," he said, but he didn't need to think about a damn thing. He wanted Jude and no one else. There'd never been anyone else for him but her.

"Hey, you two. Get your asses inside before you and that

little dog freeze to death." Tucker stood on the small porch outside the kennel.

Jude's eyes grew impossibly wider. "Tucker?"

Wade grinned. "Yeah. I thought you might want to see an old friend and maybe sit in a pile of friendly dogs."

"Sounds like heaven. Come on." She tugged him toward the building that resembled a miniature lodge where Tucker stood by the doorway and waved an arm over his head.

He followed along, Jude's statement ringing in his ears. She was right, but with only one small change. Anywhere he could be with Jude sounded like heaven to him.

19

J ude hugged Tucker tight, her head reeling from all the this-is-your-life moments that kept sending her back into the past. Tucker played a part in her memories just as much as Chet and Wade, and damn, she'd missed him.

"Holy hell, Jude. I can't believe my eyes." Tucker gripped her biceps and studied her from head to toe, a wide smile on his handsome face. "Come inside and get out of this wind."

She gladly followed him, instantly charmed by the dog kennel and she couldn't even see the pups yet. A half door separated the front area from the rest of the building. Framed photographs of the dogs decorated the room. A computer monitor and keyboard took up most of the narrow counter jutting from the wall along with a photo of a beautiful woman with a beaming little girl sitting on her lap. She picked up the picture. "Who's this?"

The smile that took over Tucker's face spoke of pure joy. "My family."

"You're married?" she squealed.

"Will be soon," Wade said. "Can't wait for the wedding, man."

"You and me both, brother." Tucker slapped a hand on Wade's shoulder and laughed. "I love Audrey like my own, but I can't wait to legally adopt her. Being her daddy's been the biggest kick of my life. You'd love her, Jude. She's smart and funny as hell."

His happiness was contagious, and she grinned. "I'd love to meet her. And your wife-to-be."

"Does that mean you're staying in town?"

Before she could answer, a big black dog shot through the doggy door and spared her a small bit of attention then hurried to Macey.

Macey's tail wagged wildly.

"Come on, Otto. Leave her alone," Wade said. "I swear these two are best buddies."

"Might as well let her off her leash," Tucker said. "She won't like being held back once we get the rest of the pups out."

Wade unhooked the leash from her collar, and she pranced to the little bed behind the counter and laid down. Otto followed like a love-sick dog and laid in front of her on the hard floor, his nose pressed against the soft bed and eyes on Macey.

Jude chuckled. "I can see who holds all the cards in that relationship."

Tucker snorted. "Usually how it goes, isn't it? The men just follow behind and hope for a scrap of attention."

Jude chanced a quick glance at Wade, who's smirk told her he agreed with Tucker.

She didn't see the parallels, but maybe that was because she hadn't said more to Wade's earlier confession than mentioning they should discuss it further. She didn't want him trailing after her with his tongue hanging out of his mouth. She wanted an open and honest conversation about how a relationship would work between them. Her time with him had ignited the flames of emotions that had smoldered for years, but was that enough?

"Anyway," Tucker said, drawing out the word as if sensing the tension. "Do you want to see the rest of the dogs?"

"Yes!"

"Otto is mine, but he comes to work with me and thinks he's the boss." Tucker pushed open the half door then kept a grip on it to let her and Wade pass through. "The others belong to the retreat."

Jude clapped her hands under her chin and melted into a pile of mush. Dogs sat quietly in their enclosures with rounded eyes trained on her. "They're all so cute. Oh my goodness, are those their names on the little mats?" she asked, pointing at a bone-shaped rug in front of one of the gates.

Tucker walked from each kennel to the next and lifted the latches for the doors. "Yep. These dogs are treated like royalty around here."

She waited for them to dart toward her, but all the dogs continued sitting even with freedom in sight. "Don't they want to see me?"

Wade laughed. "They don't do anything Tucker doesn't give them permission to do."

Once the last gate was unlatched, Tucker clapped his hands twice. "Release."

The dogs sprang forward, tails wagging and tongues lolling. A German Shepherd leaned against her knees and threatened her balance. She crouched low and hugged the black and tan mound of fur. "I think I'm in love."

Tucker grinned. "If you want them to love you back you should take them outside. I know it's a little chilly, but they need to relieve themselves. If you throw a ball a few times, you'll be their queen."

"How can I resist that?" She stood and led the pack to the door Tucker indicated.

A buzzing from Wade's pocket stalled her progress. He plucked out his phone and frowned. "I'll be outside in few. I need to take this."

She offered him a smile, letting him know he didn't need to worry about the green-eyed monster emerging this time, then stepped into the cold mid-morning air.

The dogs dispersed around her. Noses to the long blades of grass and ears twitching to the sounds around them.

Tucker ruffled the head of a Golden Retriever. "I hate why you're here, but damn, it's good to see you. You think you'll stick around after all this shit's behind you?"

She shrugged and picked up a tennis ball. "A part of me wants to hit the road as soon as I can, but another part knows I'm running from something I can never shake."

He frowned. "What are you running from?"

"My demons," she said, chucking the ball across the fenced-in yard. The dogs darted for the toy in a huge cluster.

"Those darn demons stick to you like a burr, no matter how far you run. The secret to getting those suckers to let you go is meeting them head on."

"I'm realizing that. And the first thing I need to do is make things right with my sister." She had no desire to fix anything with her father. Jenson was toxic and that would never change. The key to surviving him was separation on all levels. But her sister deserved better. Then there was her mom...

Tucker winced. "We've tried to help her. I promise, we have. But me, Chet, and Wade have all had our own fair share of shit to work out over the years and she doesn't want to hear anything we've had to say."

Her stomach knotted. "She won't want to listen to me either, but I have to try. And not just once. I need to show her I'm here to stay and will be here to help her in any way I can. In any way she's willing to accept."

A slow smile spread on Tucker's scruffy face. "So you are staying."

"I guess I am." Tingles of excitement burst inside her. After all these years, she'd finally found her way home. If she were lucky, that meant Wade was in her life for good.

The door that led into the kennel swung open and Wade hurried outside. "I have to get to the hospital."

Alarm snuffed out all the building excitement her decision created. "Is it Matthew?"

"No. My mom. She fell and needs surgery."

Her heart stuttered. Wade had already fought guilt over not seeing his mom yesterday, and now this. "Okay. Let's go. Tucker, we'll talk more later."

"Wait," Tucker said. "Is it safe for Jude to go with you? Maybe she should stay here."

The idea of being separated from Wade was like a fist to the gut. "No way. Benji's dead. Besides, Wade's bent over backwards for me since the moment I landed back in town. It's time I do the same for him. Can we leave Macey here?"

"Sure," Tucker said.

"Thanks." She captured Wade's hand and gave a decisive nod, as if to let them both know not to fight her on her decision. The trouble had passed—was dead at the bottom of a mountain road, and it was time she took her life back.

A life where she fought to right her wrongs. A life with Wade by her side.

FEAR and guilt swam together in the pit of Wade's stomach, making him nauseous. He should have gone to the nursing home first thing that morning to make sure Mama was all right. Instead, he'd been too consumed with Jude and her issues. Too focused on how to fix their problems. And because he hadn't made time for his mother, she'd been disoriented and out of sorts, causing her to fall and break her hip.

He struggled to keep his composure as he flew up to the information desk with Jude on his heels. "I need to see Velma McKenzie. I'm her son, Wade."

The older woman with round glasses and gray hair pecked the keys on her keyboard and studied her computer screen. "She'll be prepped for surgery soon but should still be in her room. Just head down the hall and turn left. Room number 13."

"Thank you." He cast a quick glance over his shoulder to confirm Jude followed then raced down the hall. Familiar faces flew by, but a singular focus pushed him forward until he reached his mother's room.

He rushed inside, the nausea in his stomach hardening to something heavy and cold. The lights were bright, and a steady beeping announced his mom's vitals.

A tall nurse with kind eyes checked the machine then patted Velma's hand. "They're almost ready for you, honey. Won't be long now. Oh, look! You've got yourself a handsome visitor."

Velma shifted in the bed to get a better look at him and beamed. "Paul? Is that you? Darlin' you didn't need to come and visit. The Chill N' Grill needs you tonight. We're too darn busy for you to step away for long."

Jude lingered in the doorway.

He didn't have time to explain how often his mother saw his father when she looked at him. Didn't have time to make sure Jude was okay. Right now, there was only one woman he could concern himself with. "You know you're way more important to me than that darn bar. I had to come and make sure you were all right. I'm so sorry I wasn't there when you needed me."

That's as much of the truth—of reality—as he could expose at the moment. Letting Velma believe he was her deceased husband was better than trying to get her to understand he was her full-grown son. That the man she'd loved was long gone, and her memories couldn't be trusted. He walked a tightrope of letting her world be what she saw and trying hard not to outright lie.

Velma waved a hand through the air. "Oh phewsh. It was just a little fall. No big deal."

Wade gripped the bed rail with one hand and rested the other on top of hers. Grief lodged in his throat. He loved his mom so damn much, and playing this role always killed him. He'd do anything for her, but not being seen by the woman who'd raised him brought pain like he'd never experienced. "We'll let the doctors decide how serious it is, okay?"

She rolled her eyes but couldn't hide her smile. "Okay. And who is this little lady hovering behind you? A new friend?"

He hesitated, unsure of how to respond. He didn't want to lie about who Jude was, but telling the truth would only confuse his mom.

"Hi, Mrs. McKenzie," Jude said. She stepped further into the room until she stood beside Wade. "I'm stopping in to see if there's anything you need. I just really wanted to see you and make sure you're okay."

"Oh, how lovely. You know, there's something about you that's so familiar. Have we met before?" She furrowed her brow as if in deep concentration, trying to place Jude's face.

Wade held his breath. How in the world was he supposed to explain Jude was his old girlfriend that Mom had known since she was a child when his mother thought he was his father?

"You've probably seen me around town. I'm a local, just like y'all. And everyone knows the best place in town to get fried chicken is the Chill N' Grill. Sometimes it feels like I grew up there."

Velma beamed. "Hearing praise like that never gets old. Paul's put his heart and soul into that place. And one day, we'll pass it on to our boy. Wade is the sweetest child, and I know he'll do right by the bar. I can tell, ya know? He's always doing what's right. Always lookin' out for his mama. I'm a very lucky lady."

A giant ball of emotion slammed against Wade, and he tightened his grip on the bed rail to keep from collapsing on the floor.

"I hope to be as lucky as you one day. With a loving family and a boy who loves me as much as your Wade loves you." Jude's voice shook slightly, the only sign she was affected by stepping into Velma's alternate reality.

He tucked her statement into the back of his mind. Did she really want a family—a son? Did she want someone to love her like him, or did she want his love back in her life? He couldn't ask her now, but as soon as he got her alone, he needed to understand what she meant.

"I'm sure you'll find exactly what you need, dear. In my experience, things always seem to work out in the end. But if you don't mind, can I have a few minutes alone with my lovely husband? I want to make sure he has a plan for what to do with me out of commission for a while, and you don't want to watch an old lady embarrass herself when I tell him how much I love him."

"Not a problem. I'll step out in the hall," she said. "I hope to see you soon."

Appreciation pressed against his lungs and stole his breath. "Thank you," he mouthed. "I'll be out in a few."

Jude walked out and leaned against the wall where he could see her if he glanced over his shoulder.

Love and gratitude spread from his chest and warmed him down to his toes. Jude's reaction to his mom—and him while dealing with her—meant more than she could ever know. And as soon as his mama was wheeled into surgery, he'd gather Jude in his arms, tell her exactly how he felt, and never let her go again.

20

Leaning against the smooth wall, Jude closed her eyes and let out a long breath. Wade might have told her his mother had a dementia diagnosis, but knowledge of her illness had done nothing to prepare her for the frail woman she'd seen in the hospital bed. Or just how far her mind could wander. Her heart shattered for Wade and the daily struggle he must endure when caring for his mama.

A twinge of regret echoed inside her. As far as she knew, her own mama was as healthy and vital as the day she'd left town. So many years laid between them. Had they been wasted or necessary for her survival? She'd always believed necessary but maybe she was wrong.

"Are you still here?"

The angry sound of her sister's voice opened her eyes and tightened her nerves. A hundred different things she wanted to say clogged her brain, all struggling to find a way out of her mouth.

Laura crossed her arms over her chest, piercing blue eyes narrowed. "Well? Why are you still here? We've been fine

without you for twelve years. You don't have to show up to cele-
brate with the family you left because your brother's finally
awake."

"Matthew woke up?" Jude asked, standing taller.

Huffing, Laura worked her jaw back and forth. "Of course
that's all you care about. He's all you've ever cared about."

The accusation cut like a knife. "That's not true. I've always
cared about you."

"Really," Laura said, her voice pitching high. "Is that why
you left me? Alone and scared and lonely in that house? That's
caring about me?"

Jude reached for her sister, but she flinched away. "I
thought I was helping you. If I wasn't there getting in trouble,
Dad couldn't use you to get to me."

Laura frowned. "What are you talking about?"

Memories of all the tears Laura had cried because of her
actions increased the pressure in her chest. "All those times he
hurt you. All those times he played mind games with you. It
was my fault. He knew hurting you would punish me more
than anything he could ever do to me. And you were so young,
so innocent. I didn't want to be the reason he went after you
anymore. I wanted to protect you. And if that meant leaving
town, then that's what I had to do."

"Do you really think the second you left town he changed?"
Laura asked with a small snort. "That he magically didn't need
to torture anyone or pull a hundred strings to make everyone
move the way he wanted them to? Because trust me, that's not
what happened at all."

The statement crashed down on her like a bomb. She
leaned against the wall for support. All those years, all those
wrong turns that led her away from her home and her friends,
and for what? She hadn't protected her sister. Hadn't gotten her
over her feelings of anger and bitterness toward her father.

Hell, she'd fallen apart at the mere sight of Jenson. Leaving might have saved her from enduring more pain and torture from her dad, but she wasn't sure if it had solved any of her problems.

"I'm sorry. I wish I could do or say something to make things up to you, but I can't. I can't change the way I left. I can't change that I wasn't there to protect you."

"I didn't need you to protect me. I needed my sister." Tears welled in Laura's eyes, and she dashed them away. "You abandoned me. He told me it was my fault. That I pushed you away. I've blamed myself for years for being the reason our family broke up, and now you've confirmed everything he said."

"No," Jude said, horrified Laura had taken on such a heavy burden at such a young age. Disgusted—yet not surprised— Jenson would shackle that burden on her. "I was young and made the only choice I thought I had. But I'd love to make up for lost time. I want to stay in Pine Valley and be here for you. Please. I want to be your sister again."

"There you are. I've been looking everywhere for you." Isaac rounded the corner, his sleazy smile growing as his wolfish eyes landed on Jude. "Well look who it is. Long time no see, Jude."

She tightened her jaw and gave a little nod. "Isaac."

He stopped beside Laura and hooked an arm over her shoulders, pulling her tight to his side. "How've ya been?"

"I'm okay," she said. "You?"

"Better now that your brother's awake. It's been a tense couple of days. You know. For the family. No one ever thought you'd come back here, but lucky for us you did and brought all your shit with you."

All the color drained from Laura's face, and she dropped her gaze to the floor. "Isaac. Don't."

He dug his fingers into Laura's flesh. "Don't what? Speak the truth?"

Laura winced. "Things are complicated and now's not the time to get into it."

His smile fell. "You're right. She's not worth our time. Come on. Your parents are in the waiting room."

"No." Laura's voice was so small Jude could barely hear it.

"Excuse me?" Isaac said, anger spewing from his words.

She licked her lips and cast a tentative glance at Jude.

Jude gave a tiny nod, doing what she could to silently urge her sister on. To give her the support she needed to stand up to her bully of a boyfriend.

"I'm taking my sister to see our brother. It's past time we're all together."

Before Isaac could argue, Jude grabbed her sister's hand and tugged her away from Isaac's death grip. "See you around, Isaac."

Laura latched on to her hand as she steered her down the hall. A ping of guilt resonated inside of her. She hadn't told Wade she was taking off, but she needed to start supporting her sister any way she could, and that meant getting her the hell away from Isaac. Even if only for a few minutes. Maybe walking away would show her she had the strength to say no, to demand respect from the people around her.

"You okay?" Jude asked.

"I don't think so but keep walking. Don't look back. He's going to be so mad." A slight tremor shook Laura's words, shredding Jude's heart.

"I won't let him hurt you. Never again."

Frowning, Laura stopped and stared wide-eyed at Jude. "How did you know?"

"Honey, I know the signs. I see the bruise you've covered under all that make-up around your eye. And we might not have spoken in years, but I know you. Can see—and recognize —the fear."

Tears streamed down Laura's face and caused tracks of black to streak over her cheeks. "I don't know what to do. Don't know how to get away from him. I feel so trapped."

"I'm here now. I want to help you in any way I can, if you'll let me."

Laura bit her bottom lip, gaze cast downward. "I... I want to believe you but I don't know if I can trust you."

Jude absorbed the blow, hating how much her decision had cost her. But right now, this wasn't about her, and she needed to step up and be the big sister Laura deserved. "Is there anyone you do trust?"

"Mom," Laura said with small shrug.

Jude couldn't stop her humorless snort. "Really? Because I don't."

Laura finally made eye contact. "She's been through a lot too, you know. Just like all of us. Dad doesn't make her life easy. Never has."

"She should have stood up to him. Should have protected us."

"Like you protected me?" Laura asked.

Jude flinched. "Fair point. But I was just a kid. She wasn't."

"That doesn't mean making tough choices has been any easier for her. You leaving...that nearly killed her. Took away any fight she had left. You broke her heart. You really should talk to her."

Now it was Jude's turn to drop her gaze to the floor. A lot of anger simmered over her mother's refusal to stand up for her, but it was possible she didn't have the whole story. And if she wanted Laura to give her another chance, she needed to be open to at least having a very difficult conversation with her mom.

A flash of Velma injured and confused entered her mind. Wade would never have another chance to get his mama back

—or at least the mama who'd raised him. She couldn't turn her back on a chance to possibly reunite with her own. "Okay. I'll talk to her, but first, I want to see Matthew."

For the first time, Laura smiled, and something shifted inside of Jude. She may not have everything in her life figured out, but she had no doubt she was home to stay.

COMMOTION AND VOICES in the hall caught Wade's attention. A quick glance showed him Jude and Laura had been joined by Isaac. He fought through the wave of anger demanding he interrupt their conversation and whisk both Jude and Laura away from that bastard. But this was Jude's battle to wage, and he had his own to fight.

"Wade?" Velma asked, stealing his attention. She blinked rapidly, as if adjusting to a shift in her reality. "What are you doing here? What happened?"

A bit of tension loosened inside him. Speaking with his mama was always a little easier when she was more aware of who he was. "You're about to go into surgery. You fell and need to get your hip fixed. Are you feeling okay?"

She furrowed her brow and the river of wrinkles creasing her forehead deepened. "No, I'm not okay. I didn't fall. I was pushed."

Her accusation twisted his stomach. "Mama, I talked to the nursing home. They said you tripped in your room. What do you mean someone pushed you?"

She gave him the same pursed lip expression she'd given him when he'd exasperated her as a child. "What do you think I mean? I mean someone pushed me. How else can I say that? And really, why in the world would I just fall down? I mean, I shouldn't be in that silly nursing home anyway. I'm not an old lady. I should be in my home with my dog and all my memories."

He deflated. Of course she hadn't been pushed. Her mind had ventured down another shaky path. He'd talk with the staff who'd worked on her floor later just to be certain, but he had faith in all the people that took care of his mom. They wouldn't put a hand on her.

A soft knock sounded at the door before the nurse stepped back in. "Okay. We're all ready. If you'll stay in the waiting room during surgery, a doctor will come out to update you as soon as possible."

Thankful for the interruption from a conversation he didn't want to have, Wade hugged his mama and kissed her cheek. "I'll see you on the other side. I love you."

She rested a palm on his cheek. "I love you, too."

He gave a small wave then stepped into the hall, allowing the medical staff the space they needed to do their job. Alarm spiked his blood pressure. Jude wasn't anywhere to be found.

Okay. Calm down. She was with Laura. She probably just went somewhere with her sister.

He'd check the waiting room first, then head to her brother's room to see if she'd stopped by to visit Brandon. With a plan made, he hurried toward the waiting area. The butterflies swarming his stomach urged him forward, his vision singularly focused on finding Jude. He rounded a corner and collided with a broad-shouldered man sporting a thick head of gray hair and slightly soft middle.

Jenson.

"Whoa there, Wade. Where are you off to in such a rush?" Jenson asked as he brushed his palms over his red sweater.

The shock of running into Jude's dad halted his motion and sent a spike of adrenaline shooting through his veins. "Sorry, sir. Just looking for someone."

Jenson snorted. "Let me guess. Jude's got you chasing after her again? I thought she'd done enough of that when you two were kids. Never thought I'd see it now. Not after she took off on all of us like she did. Do yourself a favor and don't get sucked into her drama again."

Wade didn't want to take the bait, but he couldn't help himself. "Excuse me?"

"You know what I mean." Jenson clucked his tongue. "That girl has always been a handful. Telling stories. Creating situations for dramatic flair. Always the victim. Always the misunderstood or mistreated one. Even when she ran away. It was all about attention."

Wade ran his tongue over his top row of teeth, stopping himself from punching the smug asshole in the face. "We must know two very different people. The Jude I know is kind and compassionate. She doesn't lie and she doesn't scheme."

Jenson smirked. "What kind of bull has she been feeding you this time? Clearly some sob story to make you forget about the way she left you behind. Had the whole town talking about how she broke your heart."

"She hasn't been feeding me anything, sir," Wade said through gritted teeth. "Only lifted a little mystery off things I always should have known."

Jenson's smirk melted into a scowl. "What are you talking about?"

"I know who you are and what you've done. Done to your daughters and your son and your wife. The lies you've told and the damage you've caused. Jude left to save herself, to rid herself of your toxicity. I may have been angry for a very long time, but I applaud her ability to make such a brave choice at such a young age. And just know, no matter what Jude decides to do from here on out, you'll never get to her like you used to. Never control her or torture her or make her doubt her worth."

"You don't know what you're talking about." Jenson lifted his nose as if disgusted by Wade's proclamation.

"Yes, I do, but people like you never admit their faults.

Never acknowledge the pain you've caused others. But that's your own cross to bear. Not mine and certainly not Jude's. Now excuse me, I have somewhere I need to be."

Without another look, he rushed off to find Jude, leaving Jenson Metcalf fuming behind him.

21

J ude squeezed her sister's hand as they approached their brother's room, but this time, it was to steady her nerves and not offer Laura support. The last time she'd seen Matthew, he'd been broken and battered and still asleep from surgery. She'd never forget that image.

Never forgive herself for being the reason he was in that bed to begin with. Maybe Matthew wouldn't want to see her. Maybe she'd ruined all hope of ever returning to any kind of normal life with her siblings.

Laura tugged her forward with a shy smile. "He'll be so happy to see you."

Blowing out a steadying breath, she crossed the threshold and tried to quiet the doubt swimming in her head.

"Well, look who the cat dragged in." Grinning, Matthew straightened in his bed. He threw a playing card from the cluster in his hand on the tray that hovered over the bed, the wheeled stand nestled in front of Brandon.

Brandon rose and hugged her tight before turning his affections on Laura.

"Surprised to see you two together," Matthew said, cutting to the heart of the matter like he always did.

"We ran into each other in the hall," Laura said, crossing to his side and planting a kiss on his cheek.

"And you didn't kill her?" Matthew teased.

Heat crept up the back of Jude's neck. Words escaped her, and she stared, her mouth slightly open, at her bruise-covered brother.

Laura rolled her eyes. "Don't start."

Matthew fixed his kind, brown eyes on her. "Stop lingering in the doorway. Get in here and give me a hug. It's been way too long since I've seen you."

Emotion lodged in her throat, and for the millionth time in her life, gratitude swelled inside her at her brother's ability to make her feel wanted and loved. She hurried across the room and leaned forward, falling into his open arms. Tears welled in her eyes, and she let them fall. Let herself feel safe and comforted and home.

He kissed her forehead. "It's so damn good to see you, but you're killing my side."

"Oh, no," she said, standing and covering her mouth with her hand. "I'm so sorry."

He laughed through the grimace on his scruffy face. "The pain was worth it. Trust me. I've waited a long-ass time to be in the same room as both of my little sisters."

Her mouth went dry, and she couldn't help but stare around the room and take a second to appreciate where she was. With family she loved. Who loved her back. She still had a long road to go with Laura, but at least the obstacles were gone for now. She'd find a way to move forward and repair their relationship.

"I'm sorry it took me so long to come back," she said, meaning it to her core.

Brandon pushed an extra chair next to the one he'd vacated and gestured for her and Laura to sit. "We're just happy you did.

Is Wade not with you? Does that mean the guy who beat up Matthew was caught?"

She waited for Laura to take a seat before lowering herself onto the hard cushion beside the bed. "The guy who attacked me and Matthew is dead."

"What?" Three voices rang out in unison.

She winced and held up her palms. "I don't have a lot of details yet. All I know is he was in a car accident and was found dead early this morning."

Laura reached for her hand. "Oh my God. I hate being glad someone was killed, but I'm happy he can't hurt anyone else, and the danger is over."

"Me, too."

"So what now?" Matthew asked, worry still pinching his scratched brow. "Back on the road? Another new adventure waiting for you far from Pine Valley?"

"Nah," she said, shaking her head. "I think I'll stick around for a while. Maybe forever."

"Well, isn't that nice." Her father's deep baritone echoed inside the room. He leaned against the door frame, his broad body blocking her exit.

All of Jude's muscles automatically stiffened. She darted her gaze around her, sweat dotting her hairline. The room closed in. Her heartbeat increased by the second. She swallowed hard, needing to get the hell out of there. Needing to run.

Laura tightened her grip on Jude's hand.

"Dad, now's not the time," Matthew said. The beeping on the machine hooked to him sped up.

Brandon rushed to his side and placed a hand on his shoulder, calming him.

"Time for what?" Jenson crossed his arms over his chest. "Seeing all three of my wonderful children? I need to tell your mother to get in here. She won't want to miss this. Who knows when we'll all be together again."

"No, not the time to interrupt us with your own agenda," Matthew said.

Jenson scoffed. "Agenda? I'm just a father who's happy to see everyone back where they belong. Well, mostly." He narrowed his gaze at Brandon before aiming a sickeningly sweet smile on Jude. "I always knew you'd come limping home one day. Wanting me to hold your hand and fix all your problems. Needing that attention only drama and trouble can bring."

His comment finally snapped something inside her. She summoned all the courage she had and rose to her feet, body trembling. But she wouldn't let him see her fear as she marched forward and stopped in front of him. "All I've ever needed from you is to stay the hell away from me. I made a mistake by running all those years ago. By abandoning people who loved me. I didn't know any other way to survive you and all the toxicity you brought into my life. But I'm not a child anymore. Not a little girl who doesn't know how to handle my problems. You, father, are my problem and I choose not to engage with you. Not now. Not ever. I will not let you drive me from my home or my family ever again. So please, get the hell out of my way."

Straightening to his full height, he sneered down at her. "Or what?"

She chuckled and shook her head. "Seriously? Or nothing. You have no power over me anymore so there's no reason to try." She swung her gaze over her shoulder. "I'll be back."

Smiling, Matthew and Laura nodded.

Turning back to her father, she strengthened her resolve, shoved passed him, and walked out into the hall. Leaving her bully behind her. She refused to look back, refused to see his reaction to finally standing up to him, because she didn't want to give him the satisfaction. Her cooked-spaghetti-like legs carried her quickly to the end of the hall.

A doctor in green scrubs stepped out of a room and collided with her.

The impact stole her breath. She pressed her palm against the base of her throat. "Oh my gosh. I'm so sorry."

He smiled. "No problem. I'm used to people moving fast around here. I should have been paying attention. Are you okay?"

"Yes, fine, thanks." And she meant it. For the first time in forever, her future was filled with limitless possibilities. Possibilities that could give her everything she'd ever wanted.

Frowning, he cupped his hand under her elbow. Blue eyes stared at her with concern. "Are you sure? You look a little flustered. Let's find you a place to sit."

"I appreciate your concern, but I'm good." She tried to take a step back, but he tightened his grip and yanked her closer. "You can let go now," she said.

"I don't think so," he said, keeping his jovial smile in place. "You're coming with me, Jude. And if you fight me or struggle, I'll grab my gun and kill as many people in this hospital as I can before putting a bullet in your head."

WADE COULDN'T HELP the tiny pep in his step as he hurried toward the waiting room. Confronting Jenson wouldn't erase all the pain he'd caused Jude, or even fix the problems she'd always have with her father, but it felt good to let Jenson know he wasn't fooling everyone in this town. Maybe it would be enough to keep the man in place even just a little bit.

A hopeless fantasy with a narcissist like Jenson, but at least he could continue to be by Jude's side as she battled the demons her dad had brought into her life.

Approaching the room, he studied the occupants seated in the smattering of chairs pressed against the walls. An older couple ducked their heads together and whispered in the corner, a young man with a small child kneeled in front of a coffee table and colored, and Nicole Metcalf sat with her back ramrod straight in a chair opposite him.

Her wide eyes met his and she stood, offering a weak smile as she crossed the room. Her brown slacks were perfectly pressed and not a single wrinkle marred the cobalt blue blouse. A picture of calm perfection.

But a closer look exposed the dark bags under her eyes and the tense set of her shoulders. What was her life like? Was she sad and alone, in constant fear of her husband? Or was she complicit in Jenson's behavior, her inability to stop him stemming from not caring about his actions? The questions burned his tongue, but now wasn't the time to ask.

"Wade," she said. "Nice to see you. Are you and Jude here to see Matthew?"

"Hi, Mrs. Metcalf. Actually, we came to see my mother before she went in for surgery. She fell this morning."

"Oh," she said, concern creasing the corners of her mouth. "I'm sorry to hear that. I hope everything goes okay. But where is Jude now?"

He rubbed the back of his neck. "I'm not sure. I hoped to find her here."

"Isn't she in danger? How could you let her out of your sight?" Alarm sounded from her squeaking voice.

He winced, the feeling in the pit of his stomach matching her panic. "The man who was after her and hurt Matthew is dead. But you're right, I need to find her and keep her with me until we know without a doubt trouble has passed. She was talking to Laura in the hall before they both disappeared."

"Laura was talking with Jude?" she asked, steepling her fingers at her chin. "Oh, I hope they can get past their issues. They need each other, even if they don't realize it."

Something in her tone softened him toward her. "Do you need Jude, Nicole? Do you need Laura? Matthew?"

Rearing back her head, she blinked as if she didn't understand the question. "Of course. They are my entire heart. I'd do anything in the world for them, whether they need me or not. Whether they love me or not." Her voice cracked and she wiped a tear from her cheek.

"Then show them," he urged her. "Find a way to let them see that. No matter how hard it is. No matter how impossible it may seem."

She nodded, eyes cast downward as if unable to look at him.

He debated his next move. He needed to find Jude but didn't want to leave Nicole upset and alone in the waiting room. "I'm going to check Matthew's room. Do you want to come with me?"

"I'd like that," she said, sniffing. "Thank you."

They walked the halls together in silence, his stress hitching higher with each step. Matthew's room approached, tightening the muscles in his gut. Jenson stood in the hallway. The last thing Jude needed was another argument with her father.

Jenson shifted his stance, spying Wade and Nicole, and he worked his jaw back and forth. "What are you two doing?"

"Looking for Jude," Wade said. He peered in the room, and his heart crashed to the floor. "She's not here?"

"She was," Laura said. "But she had to step out for a few."

Jenson rolled his eyes. "Always with the drama that girl."

"Enough," Nicole said, quiet as a mouse.

Jenson hiked up one eyebrow and glowered down at his wife. "Excuse me?"

"I said enough. Jude is in trouble. Not being dramatic. And now we don't know where she is. So can we please just look for her?"

Pride puffed Wade's chest, and he took a step closer to

Nicole to shield her from Jenson's clear disdain. His phone buzzed against his leg, and he plucked it out of his pocket. "Hey Cruz," he said, accepting the call.

"Where are you and Jude? I came back to the retreat to talk to you."

The urgency in Cruz's voice set Wade on edge. "We're at the hospital."

"You both need to get back here as soon as possible."

"Why?" Wade demanded. "What's up?"

"Benji Blitz's brake line was cut. He didn't get in an accident because he was injured and disoriented. Someone wanted him dead, and they made sure it happened," Cruz said. "We don't know who that person is, but chances are high that person will come after Jude next."

"Shit," Wade said, spinning in a circle to glance up and down the halls. Willing Jude to appear.

"What?" Cruz asked.

"I don't know where Jude is." Sweat coated his palms, and he avoided the curious stares of Jude's family. He had enough to worry about without explaining to them a new element of danger had just landed in their lap like a bomb.

"Well, you better find her fast before somebody else does."

22

Wind bit into Jude's cheeks as the pretend doctor escorted her out of the hospital. Walked her right out the employees' entrance without anyone aware of her plight. He kept a firm grip on her elbow, and a smile on his clean-shaven face.

He hadn't made a move for a weapon as he marched her outside, but he didn't have to. She couldn't risk him following through on the threat he'd made to open fire inside the hospital. A threat that could destroy dozens of lives. And if he was who she assumed he was—someone related to the crime family out to get her—then she had no doubt he'd have zero qualms about killing as many people as possible. Especially if that meant finally ending the job Benji Blitz had been sent to finish —her. "Who are you? Did you come to help Benji?"

He laughed, a deep and vicious sound. "Oh, I helped him all right. Now shut up and walk."

Goosebumps erupted under her leather jacket. "Did you cause his accident? Did you kill him?"

He smirked down at her before focusing on the parking lot and marching her forward.

A flash of recognition jolted her. "You're the guy in the photo I took."

He tightened his grip, digging his fingers into her flesh beneath her thick jacket.

She yelped and squirmed away from him. Having her suspicions confirmed only heighted her fear. The mafia hadn't just sent a hitman parading around as a detective down to Tennessee to kill her. The nephew whose very freedom was at stake had traveled hours to see her death through himself.

He jerked her close to his side. The smell of stale cigarettes and grease rolled off him.

Her stomach heaved. Nothing but the sound of the wind interrupted their hurried footsteps. The sky was blue, the perfect white clouds almost mocking her. Trees surrounded the hospital—a smattering of fields just beyond to one side, downtown Pine Valley a few miles south. The parking lot was filled with cars and trucks, and she was steered toward a sleek black SUV with tinted windows parked in a handicap spot in the front row.

Panic clawed at her throat. If she got in that car, chances were low she'd ever get out. If there was a good time to run, it was now. His gun—or at least the gun he claimed to have—was out of sight. Which meant if she was fast enough, she could put enough distance between them before he could secure his weapon and get off a clean shot.

She just had to figure out the best direction to go. She couldn't head toward the hospital or that would put too many other people in jeopardy. East of the building were hilly fields that would make her an open target. North was the best route. She could use the vehicles as cover as she fled into the forest. From there she could call for help.

A hard yank on her arm brought her back to the moment. "Hurry the hell up."

She tripped, kicking up a few stones and a puff of dust rose in the air.

A low growl urged her to pick up her pace as a plan formed in her mind. She had to act now. Pitching forward, she stumbled over her feet and onto the asphalt. She landed on her hands and knees. Pebbles embedded into her palms. Pain shot up her arms and she winced.

"Get up. Now," her abductor hissed.

She fisted her hands around the dirt and pebbles and dust. Jumping to her feet, she threw the debris at his face and darted away as fast as she could. Her heart galloped in her chest, adrenaline mingling with terror and making her teeth chatter. She raced for the first row of cars and ducked, sprinting toward the back of the lot.

"You're gonna regret that," he screamed.

Gulping breaths expanded her lungs. The impulse to glance behind her to see how close her kidnapper was had her fighting to keep her eyes forward. Her focus straight ahead as she passed car after car on her way to the woods.

Her phone rang, the sound startling against the quietness of the day and the curses flying behind her. She bumbled around her pocket, her hands shaking so badly, until she found her phone and pulled it out. The sight of Wade's name on the screen sent a wave of relief slamming against her.

"Jude? Where are you? Are you all right?"

Bang!

She screamed and covered her head with one hand while the other kept the phone pressed to her ear. "Wade! Help! I'm in the parking lot! There's a shooter!"

Another gunshot splintered her ear drums, the bullet collided against the side of the car beside her. She jumped, the jerking motion causing her to drop the phone, which clattered to the ground and slid under the vehicle.

Another shot. Another bullet.

She had to move. Hesitating in the parking lot made her a sitting duck, and her would-be-killer was too good of a shot to offer him a motionless target. Regret tore at her chest as she pushed forward and left her phone behind. Wade knew she needed him. Knew she needed help. Not much time had passed since she'd left the hospital. Wade could get to her. She just needed to stay alive until then.

With a renewed sense of hope, she gritted her teeth and sprinted past the last row of cars. The asphalt ended and she leapt onto green grass. Mere feet separated her from the safety of the trees where a hundred hiding places waited to shield her.

Bang!

The sound of the gun reached her as a bullet lodged into her calf. Agony burned up her leg, and she swallowed a scream. She dropped to the ground. Determination surged through her. She'd come too far to give up—had too much to lose.

The sound of heavy footsteps coming closer was like nails on a chalkboard, making her spine tingle. She clamored to her feet and limped forward. Limped toward shelter.

"You might as well give up. You'll never escape now."

"Jude! Jude! Are you still there?" Wade screamed into the phone, terror spiraling higher and higher.

Distant gunfire echoed inside the hospital room, shooting bile up his throat.

Nicole lifted trembling fingers to her lips. "Oh, my God. Jude."

Jenson coughed and shifted his weight. "I'm sure it's nothing. She's fine. She's always fine."

Laura shot to her feet. "She's not *always* fine. None of us are fine. But Jude is in trouble and that was the sound of someone shooting a freaking gun!"

Wade raced down the hall, pushing past startled nurses calming an older woman. He kept his phone pressed to his ear. "Jude? Can you hear me?"

Howling wind and the caw of a bird answered him. *Shit.* The thought of ending the only connection he had to Jude twisted his insides, but he had to call the police. He disconnected and contacted Cruz.

"Hey, man. Did you find her?" Cruz asked.

"She called. She's in trouble. Said she's in the parking lot. We heard gunshots from outside. I was by the front entrance earlier and she was nowhere around. Someone must've taken her out back." His footsteps pounded against the linoleum, each hurried step sending another jolt of panic to his heart.

"Lincoln's in town. I'll send him that way, and I'm heading there now. It will only take a few minutes. Wait inside."

"Seriously?" he shouted, rounding a corner. "You expect me to stay inside while she's out there? Possibly shot or even dead?" His voice cracked, unable to imagine a world where Jude wasn't there. Where she'd been stolen from him before he had a chance to tell her how much he loved her. How much he wanted her to stay—to stay with him.

"Dude, don't do anything stupid."

He snorted out his derision. "The only stupid thing I could do right now is leave her out there and do nothing to help her. Do nothing to let her know I'd die for her."

"So what are you going to do?" Cruz asked. "Run outside and attack a gunman bare handed?"

"Not bare handed. My rifle's in my truck." Not wanting to hear Cruz's arguments for staying put, he disconnected and raced toward the exit.

The automatic doors swooshed open. His heart pounded in his chest as he scanned the area. Jude said she was in the parking lot, but she wasn't here. Which meant she had to be in the employee parking out in the rear of the building. Grabbing his keys from his pocket, he unlocked his truck while he ran. He flung open the driver's side door and found the gun, yanking it free before rerouting to the back lot.

The gun was smooth and heavy in his hand. He turned off the safety, then trained it in front of him. An eerie silence stretched across the area. He rounded the side of the building, ears and eyes tuned to his surroundings. Should he call out? Stay under the radar?

A muffled voice turned his attention to the back of the lot. A man weaved between the vehicles. But where was Jude?

Keeping the man in his sightline and gun at the ready, he crouched as low as he could while still moving quickly toward the man.

A woman's whimper was like a tire iron to his chest. No doubt it was Jude. He couldn't think about her hurt and scared, facing down her enemy, or he'd lose his freaking mind. He needed a firm grip on his control. A firm grip on the gun. He inched closer until he was twenty feet from the man's back.

Jude lay bleeding on the ground.

Absolute horror steeled his nerves. He planted his feet and aimed the gun at the man's head.

Sirens blasted through the air.

The man cursed and pivoted in search of the intrusion. His gaze landed on Wade, and his eyes widened for a beat and a cruel smile took over his face.

"Drop your weapon. Now." Wade demanded.

"You're kidding right?" He kept his gun trained on Jude. "Make one move and I shoot your girlfriend. Again."

With the gunman's back to her, Jude kept her gaze fixed on Wade and inched away. She winced, but slowly moved through the grass toward the tree line.

Anger mixed with fear and sank low in his gut. The sirens grew closer. Tension simmered in the air. "No way you'll get away with this. The police are close. You stay a second longer and you'll have no way out of this mess. You shoot Jude, and I'll kill you."

Nervous eyes glanced toward the entrance to the parking lot.

A beat of hope pulsed through Wade's terror. Maybe his words made sense, were penetrating the thick skull of the asshole threatening to kill the woman he loved.

Flashing lights and squealing tires turned into the lot.

"Just get the hell out of here," Wade yelled.

The man tightened his jaw, his determination as clear as the blue sky. He trained his attention back to Jude.

Jude squeezed her eyes shut.

Wade steadied the gun and pulled the trigger.

The man collapsed on the ground. Blood bloomed on his side, coating his green scrubs.

Wade sprinted forward. "Jude!" He leapt around the man he'd just shot and fell to his knees beside her. Blood coated her pants and turned his stomach. She was injured and in pain because he'd left her side, but never again. He'd do everything in his power to make sure she never knew an ounce of pain ever again. "Are you all right?"

Reaching for him, she winced. Tears streamed down her face.

Agony etched on every line of her face was nearly his undoing. He struggled to hold himself together. The last thing she needed was to watch him fall apart. He cradled her jaw in his palm. "I got ya. Let's get you inside, okay?"

Moving to his feet, he scooped her into his arms. Her body was so small and frail against him.

She threw her arms around his neck and buried her head in his chest. Blood saturated her pant leg and dripped onto the green blades of grass.

Fear spiked his heart rate. He didn't know a lot about bullet wounds, but the blood loss seemed substantial. And no matter what, that couldn't be good.

A squad car peeled into the parking lot and screeched to a stop. Lincoln jumped out of the driver's side.

Wade broke into a jog. "Jude needs a doctor. Now. I shot the bastard. He's behind me."

"You what?" Lincoln asked, running toward him.

Wade lifted his chin behind his shoulder. A flash of movement caught his attention. The man on the ground rolled to his back, gun in his hand.

"Run!" Lincoln yelled and he lifted his weapon.

Wade tucked himself around Jude and covered every inch of her he possibly could as he darted forward. Terror pushed him as fast as his legs could carry him. He had to get Jude to safety. Had to keep her alive.

Bang!

Bang!

A blast of pain slammed against his back, pitching him forward. An angry heat exploded against his flesh. He struggled to keep Jude in his arms, keep himself upright. He stumbled, staggering to the side until Jude fell and he landed on the ground. Numbness encased his body.

"No!" Jude cried, crawling to him and roaming her hands over his face, his chest, his side. "Hold on for me, baby. We're going to get you a doctor. Gonna get you help. Just fight."

Her cries muffled in his ears. His eyelids grew heavy and vision blurred. He covered Jude's ice-cold hand with his and coughed, struggling to get out the words he needed to say. "I love you, Jude. I always have."

Exhaustion pressed on his chest and his eyes closed, the feel of Jude's soft lips on his was the last thing he felt before he fell into a dark pit of oblivion.

23

Doctors, nurses, and police officers raced toward Jude, their voices and concern blowing over her with the mountain wind. She squeezed Wade's hand. The last words he spoke echoing in her brain.

He loved her.

The statement should send her into a tailspin of joy, but she hadn't said it back before his eyes slid closed. Before his body went limp. Before fear fisted her lungs so damn tight she couldn't pull in a full breath.

She cradled his head in her lap, her tears falling on his face as she stared down at him. "Come on, Wade. Please. Please wake up. Come back to me. Don't let this be the end of us. Don't let him take away our future."

A gentle hand on her shoulder turned her toward Lincoln's gruff face. "Jude. We need to get you inside and have a doctor take a look at your leg."

She shook her head, the motion making her dizzy. Her leg throbbed and chills swept over her body, but she didn't care. "I'm fine. I want to be with Wade. I don't want to leave his side."

"Honey, Wade needs a doctor, too. And you need to let people do their jobs."

His words snapped her out of her stupor. She kissed Wade's forehead then reached for Lincoln, giving the medical staff the space they needed to work on Wade. "I'll be waiting for you, my love."

Lincoln looped an arm around her waist and helped her up.

She swayed, her knees buckling. Sweat dotted her hairline and she struggled to stay upright. She watched helplessly as two medical workers loaded Wade onto a gurney. His arm dangled from the side, no sign of him stirring tightened his muscles.

She covered her mouth, but nothing could stifle the sob ripping through her body.

"Hey, now," Lincoln said, keeping a firm grip on her. "Wade's strong as hell. He'll get through this. Now let's worry about you. I don't want Wade waking up and kicking my ass because I didn't make sure you were taken care of." He flicked a finger toward a nurse. "Can we get a wheelchair or something out here?"

"Yes, sir. A nurse is bringing one out right now."

A young officer with dark eyes and scruffy jawline stepped away from the body lying on the ground a few feet away.

She squeezed her eyes shut, not wanting to see the broken soul who'd cost her so much.

"I called in the coroner," the man said, his voice rough and scratchy.

She wished she could cover her ears and not even have to listen.

"Good," Lincoln said. "I'll leave you to handle everything. Jude needs medical attention before she gives her statement. I'll take that, and Wade's when he wakes up."

The strong conviction in Lincoln's tone gave her a sliver of hope she clung onto as a middle-aged man assisted her into a wheelchair and rushed her into the hospital. Lincoln stayed by her side, never leaving as the bullet wound in her calf was cleaned and stitched. An IV had medicine and fluids dripping into her, steadying her system.

"You're lucky the bullet missed the bone," the doctor said. She stripped off a pair of latex gloves and tossed them in a nearby trashcan. "The wound will be sensitive for a few days. Try to stay off your feet as much as possible. If you have to walk, I suggest crutches or a cane to keep some weight off your injured leg. For now, lay down and let the medicine work its magic."

Her calf throbbed despite the numbing cream, and she plopped back against the thin bed in the emergency room. She couldn't care less about her leg. All she wanted was news of Wade, but he'd been rushed to surgery, and she was forced to sit in a room with a doctor she didn't know and a police officer who she'd only met the day before.

"Thanks," she said, throwing her forearm over her eyes to block out the lights blazing on her face. Exhaustion weighed her down and tears pressed against the backs of her eyes. "I just want to see Wade."

"What about me instead? At least until Wade's out of surgery and you can sit beside him."

The sound of her mother's voice broke loose a dam of emotions. She sat up tears falling freely over her face, and didn't care one bit about the past or her conflicted feelings toward her mom or anything else. All she wanted was to be with someone who loved her, who could smooth back her hair and make her feel the tiniest bit better.

"I'm going to step outside and check on the crime scene," Lincoln said. "You okay? Call me or Cruz if you need anything."

Words caught in her throat, and she nodded.

Her mom took a tentative step inside, offering Lincoln a

small smile before fixing her attention on Jude. She clasped her hands in front of her. "Can I come in?"

Again, she nodded.

Nicole rushed inside and engulfed Jude in a warm hug. She ran her palm over the back of Jude's head and cooed reassuring words in her ear.

Jude clung to her mom, not realizing how badly she'd missed having her in her life. How much she needed her to step up and be there.

"I'm so sorry, baby," Nicole said, pulling back to stare into Jude's face. "My sweet, sweet girl. I should have been there for you the way you needed me to. I should have been stronger. Should have stood up in a louder way that you actually saw and heard, in a way that created change. Instead I played a part I was thrust into and didn't know how to escape, and I let your father hurt you. I hurt you. I would take it all back if I could—do it all over."

"I can't sit here and say I'm not angry," Jude said, weighing her words wisely. "Or that I can just forget everything and move forward with a clean slate. But I admit I don't know your side, and I'd like to change that. Just not now. I don't have it in me. All I want is to let my mama hold me and tell me everything's going to be okay, whether you believe that or not. Because if I admit there's any other way this could turn out, it'll destroy me."

"Scoot over." Nicole waited for her to move a bit then slid onto the bed beside her. She shifted Jude's head to her shoulder and held her close then kissed her forehead. "Everything's going to be okay. Now just close your eyes and rest while you can."

For the first time in as long as Jude she could remember, she closed her eyes and listened to her mother.

～

"JUDE. HONEY, WAKE UP."

The soft whispers of her mom floated to her, but she fought against the gentle request to open her eyes.

"Come on, Jude," her mom continued. "Wade's out of surgery."

Her eyes flew open, her pulse spiking. Disoriented, she blinked and struggled to understand her surroundings. Only one thought—one name—echoed inside her.

Wade.

"Mom?" she asked, confused by the comforting presence of her mother lying beside her.

"I'm here, baby." Nicole brushed a strand of hair off Jude's forehead. "Take a second and get your bearings."

The details of the day crashed against her, jolting her upright. "Is he okay? Can I see him?" She blurted the questions rapid fire as she stumbled over the side of the bed. A hot, angry pain shot up her leg, and she hissed out a breath.

Cruz maneuvered a chair to her side. "He's just been taken to his own room. I can wheel you down."

She nodded and fell into the chair, not even caring how long Cruz had been there or how he'd known where to find her.

Nicole swung her legs over the side of the bed and smoothed a hand over her blouse. "I'll be in the waiting room. If you want me to be."

She swallowed back tears. "I'd like that."

Cruz pushed her out of the room and down the hall.

"Is he okay?" she asked.

"I don't know anything except his room number," Cruz said.

She resisted asking any more questions because nothing would untie the knots in her stomach. Nothing except seeing Wade awake and knowing he'd survive the bullet wound that had sent him to the ground. The bullet he took while saving her life.

Pressing her hands to her abdomen, she focused on evening her breathing as Cruz turned into Wade's room. Sunlight streamed through the slanted blinds. His eyes were closed, his skin ashen.

Cruz wheeled her close to the bed. "I'll leave you two alone for a minute. Just know you're safe. The threat to your life is over. But we'll discuss all those details later. Right now, focus on Wade."

"Thank you," she choked out, waiting until he left and closed the door before skimming her fingertips up and down Wade's arm.

The machine beside him continued its steady beat.

"Hey, babe. It's me. Jude. I'm right here beside you. I promise I won't leave. Not while you're sleeping. Not once you're awake. Not after you're out of this damn hospital and back in your tiny apartment above the Chill N' Grill. I'm here for as long as you want me."

A half-smile ticked up the side of Wade's face, accentuating one dimple.

Her heart galloped in her chest and she stopped the motion of her finger along his smooth skin. "Wade?"

"Yes, darlin'?"

"Oh, my God! You're awake!" She threw her arms around his neck.

He coughed out a course chuckle and rested his palm on the small of her back. "I am. How's your leg?"

"Fine. I'm totally fine now that you're okay. I was so damn scared I'd lost you."

"It's gonna take a lot more than being shot to get rid of me." He pressed a kiss to her temple. "If you're offering to stick around, I'll accept that offer any day of the week. I'll always want you, Jude. Forever."

She gasped and reared back. He couldn't possibly mean he wanted her to be his *forever*. "Do you mean it?"

"I've never been more serious about anything in my life. I've missed you every day since you left Pine Valley. I'll spend every day showing you how much I love you. If that's what you want. If you love me, too."

"I love you more than you'll ever know. You're my best friend. My lover. My home." She pressed her lips to his, savoring the moment and thankful as hell that she'd finally found her way back to the man she'd always loved.

A KNOCK on the door interrupted the happiest moment of Wade's life—a moment he'd never thought he'd experience in a hospital bed. But he didn't care where he was. Jude loved him. She was staying in Pine Valley and wanted to be with him forever. Nothing could be better.

Cruz stepped inside. "Sorry to interrupt. Hope that was enough time for privacy, but I have some information."

No amount of time alone with Jude would have been enough, but Cruz was right. A lot had happened, and he had to know where everything stood. Starting with his mother. "Is my mama out of surgery?"

Cruz nodded. "She is. Everything went well, but there's one thing you need to know."

Alarm hummed inside him, and he tightened his hold on Jude. "What is it?"

"Your mom was pushed at the nursing home."

He squeezed his eyes shut against the statement. His mom had told him someone had pushed her, and he'd swept it under the rug, blaming her confused mind. "She tried to tell me. I didn't believe her."

Wincing, Jude shifted to sit on the side of his bed and rested a palm on his chest. "You had a lot thrown at you in a short amount of time. You can't beat yourself up for this, especially since the truth came to light."

He opened his eyes and stared at her beautiful face. Gratitude swept over him. "You're right. But who pushed her?"

"The same man who took Jude and shot you. He must have done his homework and knew if your mom was in the hospital, you'd show up and Jude would be with you," Cruz said.

His stomach churned. He'd been played and put Jude's life in danger. Not to mention his mom had been at risk. "How did you figure this out?"

"One of the nursing aids at the care facility looked at the security footage and alerted authorities. Lincoln connected the dots when he showed up here."

"I can't believe someone would be so evil," Jude said. "I'm so sorry your mom got pulled into my mess."

"You didn't do anything," Cruz said. "A criminal broke into your life and hijacked it for a bit. What he chose to do is on him. Not you. And luckily, everyone made it out in one piece. But it's over."

Jude sucked in a large breath. "Are you sure?"

"Yeah, I spoke with Detective Hocking. The nephew you photographed is the guy who Lincoln shot and killed, but a warrant got her team into his apartment. They found enough evidence to throw the whole family behind bars."

"Wow, I can't believe this is really over." The noose of tension around his neck disappeared.

"Yep, and now all you two have to worry about is your recovery," Cruz said. "Glad to see you're both going to be okay. Now if you'll excuse me, I need to head down to the station and look after some paperwork."

Wade waited for him to leave the room before pulling Jude close to his side. "Lay with me."

"Is that okay?" Jude asked. "I don't want to hurt you."

"I don't care." He held his arm open, and Jude nestled

against him. "Nothing hurts when I have you with me. Plus, the pain meds aren't too bad either."

"Is it weird I'm grateful I took those pictures?" she asked.

He entwined his hand in hers and kissed her knuckles. "And why do you think that is?"

"I've traveled a million miles and those photos led me right back here to you. I regret leaving the way I did, but I don't regret the woman I am today because of it. Because I know without a shadow of a doubt I am where I belong. Right here with the man I love."

Wade's heart filled with joy as everything he ever wanted fell into place. "I love you too, Jude. Always have. Always will."

EPILOGUE

Grimacing, Wade tightened his grip on the handrail as he struggled to climb the stairs to his apartment.

Jude hooked her arm around his waist. "You should have let me call someone to help you get upstairs."

"Just a couple more steps. Almost there." He held his breath and took the final step onto the small landing then handed Jude the key. He braced a forearm on the wall and drips of sweat fell from his temple. "Go ahead and open it. I need a second."

With her arm still looped around him, she opened the door and helped him to the couch.

Exhausted, he plopped onto the soft cushion. "I'm sorry, babe. You're nursing your own injury. You're right. I should have had someone else help me."

"Don't worry. Now that we're upstairs, I don't plan on leaving for days. Give us plenty of time to recuperate together." She curled beside him and placed a kiss on his cheek. "Our life together is going to be amazing if you keep repeating those words."

He frowned. "What words?"

She grinned. "The ones that admit I'm right."

Her teasing tone eased all his discomfort. "I'll remember that. I gotta say though, I wish I could bounce back as fast as you."

"I didn't have a bullet lodged in my back. You're lucky you got out of the hospital after only a week. Hell, you're lucky you're still able to walk. And how cute is it that you and your mom will have the same physical therapist?"

He snorted out a laugh. "Adorable. I'll be surrounded by little old ladies for weeks. Which reminds me, can you grab my black backpack from the hall closet?"

She wrinkled her nose. "How did physical therapy remind you of a bag in your closet?"

He shrugged and struggled to keep from grinning. This was not how he ever planned for this moment to go, but he didn't care. Recent experience had shown him life was way too short —too fragile—to ever let anything pass him by. To not seize every single opportunity to find happiness.

And right now, the only plan he needed was to make this the happiest day of his life.

"It's weird not having Macey here. I can't wait for Chet to drop her off later," Jude said as she fetched the bag and tossed it into his lap, anchoring her fists on her hips. "Now what's in that thing you just had to get your hands on as soon as you got home from the hospital?"

"Patience, please." He unzipped the front pouch and found the little black box his mom had given him right after her diagnosis.

"Oh my gosh," Jude said, covering her mouth with shaking hands. "Is that what I think it is?"

He flipped open the lid and grinned, his heart threatening to beat out of his chest. "I always dreamed of getting down on one knee in front of you with this ring, but I'm gonna need you to help me out a little and come sit beside me."

"Okay," she said, her breath wispy. She sat and faced him, tears shimmering in her eyes.

"Jude, I love you more than life itself. All my best memories include you. All my dreams are centered around our life together. You are my past, my present, and future. Will you be my wife and let me love you every day for the rest of my life?"

"Yes," she said. "One thousand percent yes. Never in a million years did I think I could be lucky enough for you to still love me—still want me. I can't wait to be your wife."

He plucked the solitaire diamond from its plushy pillow and slipped it on her finger. "This was my mom's ring. She wanted me to give it to someone I loved as much as she loved my dad. She may never understand how much I love you or know that we found our way back to each other, but I want to believe that deep down she always knew I'd give this ring to you one day."

Jude tucked her thumb under his chin and drew his face inches from hers. "She knew, honey. Everyone's always known we were meant to be together forever. Today and every day I choose you."

"I choose you, too." He captured her mouth with his and sealed their future with a kiss.

Thanks for reading Crossroads of Innocence. The Injured
Heroes Series continues in an exciting crossover with Janie
Crouch's Zodiac Tactical Series. Grab CODE NAME: GEMINI
here! https://readerlinks.com/l/3388197

ACKNOWLEDGMENTS

I can't believe the sixth book in this series is done. It feels like just yesterday I came up with the idea for the Injured Heroes Series. It has taken a village to make these books, and I have to say, I'm lucky to have such an amazing one that supports me daily.

A big thanks to my husband and children. You guys stand by me no matter what, and that means the world to me. Thanks to my awesome critique partners, Samantha Wilde and Julie Anne Lindsey. I couldn't survive a day without your insight and friendship.

Much gratitude to The Editing Soprano for making my words shine, and for the team at Deranged Doctors for designing another beautiful cover.

And mostly, to all my readers. I hope you enjoyed Wade and Jude as much as I did!

Until next time!
Danielle

ABOUT THE AUTHOR

Danielle M Haas is a stay-at-home mom turned author. When she isn't writing fast-paced romantic suspense novels with mysteries to live for and romance to die for, she's busy being a taxi driver to her two busy kids and forcing her introverted self to talk to other soccer moms. Her kids and husband are her world, which is also shared with her hyper Bernie doodle, two sassy cats, and one leopard gecko who's happy to chill on a rock all day. Her days are packed with cuddles, kisses, and a brain constantly thinking of new ways to create danger and romance for her next book.

ALSO BY DANIELLE HAAS

www.ingramcontent.com/pod-product-compliance
Lightning Source LLC
Chambersburg PA
CBHW060327260626
47160CB00007B/2706